The Ghost's Daughter

Martina Mercer is an award winning writer of many published short stories and poems. She is currently adapting her first book, *Serial First Dater*, for television. She has had many jobs in her time, but all have been secondary to writing. She has a BA(hons) in English literature and a collection of writing awards from as early as nine years of age. As a grownup she lives on a small holding with her two children, adoring husband, a ferocious French cockerel and a dog named Banana.

ALSO BY MARTINA MERCER

Serial First Dater (currently being adapted for television)

The Sins of the Next Generation (coming summer 2010)

Details of poetry and other short stories can be found at www.martinamercer.com

The Ghost's Daughter

Martina Mercer

Published in 2010

Copyright © Martina Mercer 2010

Martina Mercer has asserted her right under the Copyright, Designs and Patents Act, 1988 to be identified as the author of this work

The novel is a work of fiction. Names and characters are the product of the author's imagination and any resemblance to actual persons, living or dead is entirely coincidental.

This book is sold subject to the condition that it shall not, by way of trade or otherwise, be lent, resold, hired out, or otherwise circulated without the publisher's prior consent in any form of binding or cover other than which it is published and without a similar condition including this condition being imposed on the subsequent purchaser.

First published in 2010

ISBN 978-1-4452-7907-7

The Ghost's Daughter

For Dad, you may be gone but your wisdom lives on....

The Ghost's Daughter

Martina Mercer

The End of the Beginning

My supernatural instincts first reared their dusty moth-eaten heads when I turned the tender age of five. I could just hold a decent conversation, see people's faces if I stood on a chair, and kick their ankles if they would not listen.

I was a skinny little waif in bunches and dungarees. Tough as nails. Therefore, the strange old man with a beard, standing at the top of our staircase one morning did not faze me one bit.

"I'm angry!" I shouted.

I plonked myself on the top step, and looked up at his long face. He did not smell of anything, yet he looked like he should. His tweed jacket was threadbare, his beard a dirty blond. Not fashionably dirty but really dirty, bits of discarded food and everything.

"I'm Jack." He smiled.

"I want to go to the shop! I want some jelly teddies but I've no one to go with!"

He crouched down to my level, only then did I notice his feet were naked.

"Come with me," he whispered. He held out his hand and we began walking down the wooden staircase. The huge glass panelled oak front door was only feet away across the tiled hall. Soon we would be heading towards the tiny corner shop. I would be purchasing my heart's desire. My ten pence pocket money had been burning a hole in my pocket for the last hour.

"Tina James just WHERE do you think you are going?"

Oh dear, Mummy.

"The shop. I've someone to go with now!" I shouted, defiant and proud.

"Who?" she asked curiously.

"Mister Jack. Here look. He is taking me. He said he'll take me!"

"But Tinsey, Tinsey, there's nobody there."

I look up at Mister Jack; he looks down at me, then across to my mother. He shrugs his shoulders, he keeps moving as if we are going to walk straight through her. I have to stop walking; I am almost standing on her toes. I point to him, furious that even with her nose touching his ear; she's still pretending not to see him. I stamp my feet and scream. I can't hold back the tears.

"He's here! Right here!" Except he's not. He has let go of my hand and has continued his stroll, disappearing into thin air before reaching the door.

My mother pulls me to her chest and holds me.

"Ok darling, ok. Look, you should not be going to the shops with strangers anyway."

"He's NOT a stranger. He's JACK!"

"Ok, ok, look I'll take you to the shops, OK? Come on."

I nattered about Jack for weeks. I would often bump into him at the top of the stairs and I would sit on the top step and tell him my five-year-old worries. My brother, Luke, pinching my toys; wanting a puppy for Christmas; Marie Ann pulling my bunches in class. Each encounter ended the same, he would walk down the stairs and disappear. Every time, against mother's wishes, I tried holding the door open for him, holding onto his hand to see if he would take me along but he never did. He became quite a fact of life. Until one day, when the kitchen extension was finally finished and our newly renovated house, my home for the last eighteen months was put up for sale. The Americans call it flipping that always makes me giggle. As luck would have it though that was not the end of Mister Jack, as it sold within days to the parents of my school friend, Timothy.

I cried when I left Mister Jack and I begged Timothy to take care of him. Timothy spread silly rumours that I was crazy, that I talked to myself, that I needed to be put on a funny farm. The joke, the karma, took only twelve months to boomerang right back at him. I love Karma. Out of the blue, he returned home from school to find a priest, scattering holy water, whilst his mother followed with a burning bush. I later discovered this would have been sage. Regardless of all that, his mother had called an exorcist. Ha ha Timothy! It seems the kitchen extension had been built onto an old railway track and many moons ago, Jack had lost his life whilst constructing the track, simple dehydration and overwork was the cause. Many railway workers had met their end the same way. The exorcist advised a radical plan of taking away the thousand-pound extension. This was the early eighties, a thousand pounds was a lot of money but Timothy's mother did not hesitate. Although she could not see Mister Jack a feeling of unease, a whisper she could not catch, surrounded her. The rumours about me stopped, and my five-year-old self accepted along with fate and destiny, that supernatural, superstition, signs and spookiness were a normal part of my life.

So I will bring you back with me to present day, and tell you that I should be prepared for the knocking on my door right now. Since that first encounter, I have been shown every sign, pointed directly in this direction. The future has been made completely obvious to me, and yet despite the foresight, I chose to ignore it. I was hoping that just for once, they could be wrong. I believed, if I buried my head in the sand, it would go away. The noise from the door becomes louder. A huge banging. The knocker is defiantly using something other than their fists. The walls shake with it. My stomach churns. It is deathly dark, and nine pm.

On a lighter note, in daylight hours, I own a little bookshop. My father helps with the stocking. An antique dealer himself, he has the contacts. I love my little shop, and my shop loves me. Only last week, a box of rare and second-hand crossed my threshold. Not unusual. Daily in fact. On the top of this box, however, was a book written by the families of Dunblane victims. The ones left behind.

Generally, I am extremely superstitious, you will see. I do not enjoy reading of death, grief, tragedy. I do not enjoy depressing music. It still surprises me that Westlife do not have a mini contract in their CD covers, a disclaimer you should sign so families can't sue their bums off if you happen to slit your wrists whilst listening to their music. It'll come. Along with the pledge.

Anyhow, this book screamed at me, not literally. Lucky enough to not having dealt with much living grief, at all, something urged me to pick it up, to turn the closed sign around on the door, and sit next to my little log fire in the store room and read.

I read of losing children, husbands, wives, and then, when I read an account of losing parents I stopped and my mind wandered.

"Just how would I feel if I lost a parent?"

I considered it for a while, thinking first of mum, then dad, tears streaming down my face. This train of thought completely alien to me. I'd usually push it aside as quickly as it arrived. Inviting the devil in, my dad would call it. No good will come of thinking like that. However, even then, with my twenty-three years of experience in all matters supernatural, I knew this train of thought was not morbid nightmares; this was another force preparing me, as gently as it could. Now, the knocking was the fruit of its labours, and I know my world is about to be turned upside down in an instant.

My son has slept all afternoon, and I let him. Another sign. He is nearly three years old; he's climbing behind me on the sofa dressed in a fleecy all in one psychedelic green suit, without feet. He looks cuddly, but his nappy's heavy and his eyes wide open.

"Gan Dad, Gan Dad, Gan Dad!" He shouts, he races to the window, we're above the shop, and he looks for Dad's white van but see's nothing. Since Mickey's father left us to travel the world with his band, Dad has taken on the role of male role model, and he fulfilled it well. Mickey loves him, with a passion. The feeling was mutual. It wasn't Dad at the door though.

Dad wouldn't have given me a talk only yesterday if it were him. He wouldn't have harvested his cherry tomatoes with Mickey only this morning, if it were him. Dad wouldn't have rang and asked me not to go for dinner, for the first time in his entire life, if it was him. Dad wouldn't have mentioned the hundreds of crows that had settled on the roof of their new house, if it was him.

Dad knew, dad had the same intuition, he warned me, and I'd be almost prepared if I'd been paying enough attention. The one thing I do know though is as soon as I open the door, I will never take another person I love for granted ever again.

With Mickey still peering out of the window, his chubby palms flat against the glass, I go downstairs, and gingerly open the back door. It's not a giant, not a monster, not a gaggle of policemen with a battering ram, it's mum. Her hair is soaking wet, she has slippers on her feet. She has a manic air about her, which, before you ask, is not commonplace. My mum is quite sane.

"He's DEAD!"

There we have it, that's it. I've been expecting it, I knew it was coming. I've thought about it. Planned what I was going to do, but nothing, no instinct, no intuition, no spookiness, no coincidence, has prepared me for this devastating blow. A sledgehammer would have been gentler. In fact, I'd welcome one right now, so I didn't have to feel.

My bowels go first. I rush to the bathroom. Instant diarrhea. Then vomiting. I find it strange that even the most realistic of films have told of the vomiting, but nowhere have I seen the leading lady rushing to sit on the loo when given devastating news.

When, only a few minutes later, I pull myself together, I find mum pacing the living room. She keeps picking Mickey up, then putting him back down; he thinks it is a game.

"How?" I ask.

Mum looks at me as if seeing me for the first time. My head begins to pound.

"Heart attack I think. He was fine, happy; we were just about to have curry and chips. He couldn't catch his breath and..."

"Where is he now?"

"The ambulance took him; they were trying to revive him as they pulled away."

"So he could still be alive?" Hope, there always has to be hope.

"No Tinsey, small, tiniest possibility, no, trust me."

I'm not listening, I'm pushing mum out of the door, a possibility. That's good. Surely, we deserve a break. He's still alive. Heart attack, people have them every day and survive, why not Dad?

I know why not Dad. You don't, so I will elaborate. On Dad's fiftieth birthday, he told me this was going to happen!

He had accompanied me to a book fair, a first for both of us. The roles had been reversed for a day, as it was I who usually played the role of assistant at various antique fairs around the UK and Europe. Often we'd set off at 5am in a van that had seen better days. We would have camp beds slotted between the furniture in the back. Our home for the extended weekends. Sometimes scorching, more often than not freezing cold, with icicles dripping from the ceiling of the van, our makeshift bedroom. From as early as I can remember we'd have a small tot of whisky in our morning cuppa to stave off the bitter winds. We'd revel in the hand driers in a local supermarket. Dad would cook fat brown sausages over a tiny camp stove, a chunk of golden butter, fresh white bread and a sachet of brown sauce. Rocking horse he called it, with his rhyming slang. We'd feast, laugh, drink and dance from start to finish. Returning exhausted and needing a good weeks rest. The best of days. It meant a lot, and showed the changing times, when Dad said he'd like nothing better than to spend his fiftieth birthday helping at my first fair.

"So, how does it feel to be fifty Dad? Not half as bad as expected?" I ask, and he smiles at me, the huge smile that spreads from ear to ear, yet his eyes are sad.

"Twice as worse. Like a thunderbolt. BANG. Fifty. BANG. Life over. Just like that." He looks to the distance. Always strong. Always dependable. Always tough. It takes a minute to realise his words are the exact opposite.

"Why? Don't be daft. It's a number, that's all. Just another day. No different to yesterday."

"I keep telling myself just that. Just before I met your mum, a gypsy stopped me; I was skeptical at first, until she speedily detailed my entire life with bullet points. Her parting shot cost me sixpence. That's all. You will die at the same age as your mum."

We don't often talk about Dad's side of the family much, but I know Dad's mum died before I was born.

"She was fifty." he finishes.

A customer picks up a second edition of Black Beauty, we never return to the conversation. It's difficult to talk to Dad about his emotions. He's an excellent listener, fantastic with advice, fabulous for a chat, but for him to open up showed weakness. Dad didn't do weakness. As a daughter, I was glad of this. I wrongly assume Dad has the birthday blues. That a gypsy's predictions would mean nothing to him every other day, a defender of the free lunch proverb.

My first regret, I should have asked more.

Mickey poking me in the eye brings me back to now. I have promised to wait for Aunty Sally to pick me up, mum doesn't want me driving in my state, agreeing was the only thing I could do to make sure mum left. We're both at a complete loss, and mum doesn't want her suspicions confirmed. Waiting seems like an attainable feat, considering everything else, however, it takes precisely ten paces and one minute of foot tapping before I'm changing Mickey's nappy, and heading out of the door with my car keys. I need to be with Dad. Somebody, some other force, has other ideas. For the first time since renting the shop and house, a strange yellow Nissan has parked across my drive. Completely blocking in my little Yaris. I look up and down the road, Mickey minus socks on my hip, I see the Salvation Army has lights on and doors open, so I run across.

I enter the modern church to a congregation of people singing, all gleefully, celebratory and instantly anger hits. How on earth can these people be smiling, laughing, singing when the most important man in my life may be dead? How?

I compound my rage into my voice box and shout.

"WHO THE HELL PARKED A YELLOW FREAKING NISSAN ON MY DRIVE?"

The people shake their heads in unison disgusted by my outburst, Mrs. Sharp, a regular customer of mine breaks through her pew length, and steers me towards the open door.

"You can't do this dear." She patronizes, " We are celebrating. You just can't do this. A car is not such a big problem. Go home."

"It IS a big problem when I need to be somewhere. My father could be dying, and I can't get to him."

Mrs. Sharp has a crush on my father. Most women over thirty did. She thinks I'm overreacting. Fit, muscled man, dying? Surely not.

"You're in no state to drive anyhow. Seems the Nissan owner is doing your father a favour, he doesn't need to be worrying about you too. Let's ring a taxi."

She's talking too slow for my mind that is speeding ahead. I need to walk it out, pace it out, shout it out, and drive it out.

"I'll do it, forget it, my mistake, I'll do it." Seems customer service is completely forgotten when a life hangs in the balance.

I run back, Mickey still on my hip, and enter the shop. The lights are all off bar the display in the window. I use the phone near the till, as it gives me a perfect view of the road should Aunty Sally turn up.

After the third taxi firm promising transport within the hour, I realise its Saturday night. Prime Time. I've no chance. I run up and down the drive again, for effect, to no avail. The garish Nissan is still sat there. I kick its wheels, Mickey laughs. The phone ringing from the shop stops me ripping the handles off the doors. I'm frantic.

I turn the lights on and put Mickey on the floor next to the children's section. He makes light work of emptying shelves I've agonised over. I don't care. I pick up the phone, it's my brother Luke

"You need to be with mum. Right now. Get to her."

"I'm trying; I'm bloody trying, only option left is to wait for Aunty Sara."

"Ring a bloody taxi, just get there."

I'm about to argue that I already have when a thought occurs to me.

"You've spoken to mum?"

"Of course."

"When? Where did she ring you from?"

"The hospital."

"So Dad, How's Dad, you'd know, you know!"

"He's going to be fine, just get there."

I drop the phone, and sit on the floor. Without a shadow of a doubt, I know Luke just lied to me. He gave nothing away, yet my instinct tells me I'd feel it if Dad were still alive. I'd know. I am certain, absolutely certain that he isn't. I've missed what I was pacing for. The nervous energy, the jumpiness, the jitters, I needed to be there, to do something, to help. I'd missed it. Now he was gone. I bury my wet face in Mickey's thick hair as a pair of headlights stop directly in front of my window display. The cavalries arrived.

Chapter 2

Aunty Sara jumps out of her hire purchase purple Corsa, looks myself and Mickey up and down, and then tugs at my arm.

"Uncle Pete's in the car, come on, let's get to the hospital."

I follow on autopilot, each sense already shutting down. This is a sure defence mechanism, my minds way of preventing additional pain. I'm looking through a fog, hearing only instruction. I take a seat in the back, and cuddle Mickey to me. Uncle Peter nods a greeting but he can't look me in the eye.

As Aunty Sara drives, she mumbles.

"If you want to bury, you'll need a green form."

Some part of this reaches me, I may have given up, yet there was still a sliver of hope, I could still be wrong. I was most definitely not ready for everyone else to give up. That would make it real. I can't handle real. Instinct is changeable, untouchable, and arguable.

"Bury? He's not dead!"

Aunty Sara swivels in her seat, as she does, the car veers off the road, the tyres skimming a huge pond, as a tree looms, and Uncle Peter grabs the wheel. He swears at her, quite a bit. She slams on the brakes, and apologises, a lot. I don't think hitting the tree would have cleared the fog from my head; I really couldn't be any calmer if I'd swallowed a full bottle of Valium.

"I'm sorry Tinsey, so sorry, but I thought..."

"No, you're wrong, I sent mum after him on the ambulance, and they were still trying to revive him. People survive heart attacks every day."

There's no infliction to my voice, complete monotone. Mickey is sat oblivious to all of it, no whinging, crying, slapping, and poking. He knows something's afoot and is waiting patiently for events to unfold.

"In that case, let's speed up, come on."

I can tell Uncle Peter would have cursed much more if I'd not being a passenger, I go a little way to understanding Aunty Sara's constant nervousness.

The next bend, and the signs point in the direction of the hospital, I let my mind wander and think back to the day before, the last time I saw Dad.

The atmosphere had been touchy to start with. A week previously, we'd argued, for the first time as adults, ever. I'd been absolutely riddled with PMT, Dad was hot and rushed. We argued over nothing, it was my fault, and then for four whole days we didn't speak. It was agony. We were both too stubborn to make the first move, so this was tentative. Mickey had missed my Dad a lot in those four days; I had felt as though my arm had been sliced off. Looking back, I see, it was nature's way again of preparing us for a life without him. I don't think it helped. At all.

So yesterday, only twenty-eight hours ago, Dad walked into my shop. He'd ambled the two miles from home to here. I'd usually congratulate him on the exercise; however, he didn't look any better for it.

"I'll get you a cup of tea Dad."

"No, no, you're busy, I'll get my own. Not stopping long, just wanted to see you."

"I'll be as quick as I can."

My business manager was in for a meeting, and boy, did she go on. Usually, I'd enjoy the company; adore having someone to rattle on to about my baby, my business, today though, as soon as Dad walked in, I was eager for her to leave. She just wasn't taking the hint.

Half an hour later she leaves, I take myself through to the back room, I want to spend some time with Dad, and I've missed him.

"Cup of coffee for you here," he points. He smiles sheepishly.

"Cheers Dad, nice to see you. I'll drive you back." The bell on the shop door rings, indicating a new customer, I curse.

"Look, I know you're busy, it's brilliant, don't let me stop you, I'm quite happy here."

"But I want to talk to you."

"You've a business to run, I'm not going anywhere."

The urge to walk through to the shop and tell whatever customer it was to fuck off, was overwhelming. I put the feeling down to not seeing Dad for a little while, but I know if it were Brad Pitt I'd have kicked them out to spend an hour alone with Dad.

It wasn't Brad Pitt. It was Les. Forty years old, bookshop entrepreneur. Has the monopoly of North Yorkshire with second-hand paperback shops. An absolute darling. Tiny weenie huge crush on myself, and in my darkest moments I have considered it, however, I like my men a little meatier than this wiry, bespectacled, tall middle-aged cookery book collector.

"I'm a bit busy Les, some other time?"

"Busy, how?"

"Well, got my dad here, want a cuppa with him."

"Your Dad's here every day. Hello MIKE!"

Dad shouts from the back room, "Don't let me stop you."

Bugger.

Les takes Dad literally. I buy some books from him; we discuss what's hot and what's not in used paperback land, every time I try to cut the conversation short he pitches in with another subject. I'm becoming a little resentful of him outstaying his welcome. I make a point of looking at my watch for the umpteenth time, and on the last occasion I see where the hands are pointing. I'm due to pick up Mickey from the childminders in half an hour. I turn the sign on the door, ask Les to leave, and finally sit down to my coffee, which is still remarkably hot. I smile when I think Dad may have had something to do with it.

Dad's been sat, all this time waiting patiently. I'm still agitated that our time together, has been spent. I try to tell myself we can try again Monday, yet this thought isn't penetrating, or indeed bringing any comfort.

"I need to pick Mickey up Dad, and I wanted to talk to you."

"What about?"

"Nothing really, just this and that."

"You shouldn't need me anymore, you've done it. Look at you today, I'm proud, all by yourself, you've built this up, no help from anyone. You've done it. I taught you well."

"You did, and you've helped. So much. You have."

"With your knowledge, what I've taught you, what you've learnt yourself, you should never be skint, ever."

"I hope not. Will you come with me to get Mickey? He's staying with you anyhow. I'm out, with Gray and Gav."

"No, drop me off at home though please, let your mum pick Mickey up, I need an hour's kip."

"You look like you do. What's the matter?"

"God knows, thought I'd walk it off, but I haven't."

"Doctor?"

"I hate them, as you know, but I did go. He said indigestion."

"You need to go back. Immediately."

I know he won't. Dad hates feeling like a hypochondriac, even worse, being accused of being one. Typical man. He nods to amuse me. I should have done more.

During the ride in the car we talk about my future, mortgages, which collectibles to sell, which to hold onto, where to take the business. I leave Dad feeling as if my next few years are mapped out, if only I stay on the correct path.

His parting words, "just don't marry."

"Why? You did."

He laughs that big booming laugh that bounces off walls. Infectious. I feel giddy that I've made him happy and I laugh too.

"It benefits me, I'm a man. A man can't go far wrong getting married, especially my generation. You, you've too much to lose. Your identity. Yourself. Save it. Have fun. You've got Mickey; you don't need some idiot running your life for you. Telling you what to do and when."

"They might not. They might let me lead my own life."

"If you were ugly, maybe, but you're not. The song, "when you're in love with a beautiful woman?" Listen to it."

"OK. Just fun."

"Good girl. Play the field. Let them spoil you."

I pull onto their drive and Dad steps out of the car. He waves with his right hand while he walks into the house. Mum's not back from work yet, she'll be picking Mickey up from me en-route. I don't feel like it's a farewell at this point. If I did, I'd be running after Dad and holding on to him for dear life, but I don't. I feel we've reached a milestone, I feel as if today I've gained my Dad's respect in a business sense. That he's proud I've turned out as he wanted me to, with the shrewd cool head he'd taught me. That he can worry a little less knowing I was in control of my own destiny. That's it, a milestone. A shift in our relationship. Not complete devastation of, no way.

I continued with my evening surrounded by a skin of pointlessness, Gavin and Grey were fantastic, I played my role of fag hag stupendously well despite the aura, yet when Grey told me of his stepfathers demise from the mortal realm only two weeks previously, I laughed.

I'd never laughed over another's death before. The fact that Grey laughed along with me was not a point we shall dwell on, it was wrong. To take life so flippantly, and death so naturally.

Grey's stepfather was an absolute abusive twat mind, but all the same. It was wrong. From that point on, try as I might I could not get drunk. Vodka after vodka. I was so infuriated with myself for not being at the slurring words stage by eleven pm that I called a taxi. These evenings few and far between, no need to ruin the lie in with a hangover for nothing now. It was this twist of fate, which meant I woke bright eyed and bushy tailed, instead of with a 24-hour hangover, that was usually the case.

Therefore, Saturday was chill day. Mum dropped Mickey off, I was supposed to be helping Dad with a fair in the morning, which usually meant staying over at Mum and Dad's, all the better for leaving Mickey with mum, as Dad gleefully dragged me out of bed at silly o'clock in the morning. I enjoyed it usually, but this time, just this once, the words tumbled out of my mouth before I could stop them. I told mum I'd rather not go.

Dad was waiting at home for the chimney sweep and the carpet fitters.

As soon as I'd told her, the brick of a mobile phone in her hand began to ring.

I busied myself cuddling Mickey, checking his nappy as she talked.

"That was Dad," she announced, "I better go, he doesn't know which rooms I want doing with the carpet."

"Ok, did you tell him about tomorrow?"

"Yeah, he's disappointed, but says it's probably for the best. We need to leave a parking space for the Chimney sweep, and now the TV aerial people."

"Aerial?"

"Hundreds of crows landed on the roof, your father got the shotgun. Raced up a ladder to scare them all away. They took the aerial with them!"

"Blimey. Bloody things."

"Quite. Right, I'm off. I'm shattered. The little monkey, he won't sleep for me. Kept coming down climbing on your dad's knee for a cuddle."

Dad not being the most affectionate of creatures, I can see how this made today's family news.

"He thinks he's his Dad. He is really. The closest he's going to get for a long time."

"True, well, your Dad was over the moon I could tell. So, they had a bath. Lots of splashing, playing. Mickey was over excited then. Wanted to play all night. Your Dad didn't help. Like two kids they were."

"You could probably do without us tonight then?"

"To be honest, yeah. Your dad could do with a good rest too before morning, so it works out for the best. You know where we are if you need us though."

With that mum left, just as the shop phone rang. Mickey was trying to count some tomatoes he'd brought home in a Bob the builder hat.

Dad was on the phone.

"Your mum still gabbing?"

"No, she's just left."

"You ok? Mickey shown you the tomatoes?"

"Yeah, he's counting them."

"He's done well; he's wanted to pick them all summer. We harvested them this morning. Been a long wait for the poor little sod."

"I know. How are you after those crows?" I'm laughing.

"Oh Tinsey, you wouldn't have bloody believed it. Poxy bloody things. Like a Hitchcock film it was!"

"Mum told me. Are you ok about tomorrow?"

"Yeah, I don't know if I'm going myself yet. Bit knackered. I don't know where you'd park anyway. Leave it for today, and then come for dinner tomorrow night, yeah?"

"Course."

"Ah, your mum's here now. Look after yourself, and if you need us, you know where we are."

"I'm just going to crash Dad, good film, playdo, you know the drill."

"I don't blame you. Me too."

Little did I know the end of that conversation was setting the foundations for a most extraordinary beginning?

Chapter 3

We finally pull up outside the hospital, Aunty Sara, although nervous, is worried about parking in the emergency bay. I need one of them in the front to move before I can exit with Mickey. Now I'm here, my impatience is forefront. Insurmountable. Like a child, I'm banging the back of Uncle Peter's seat with my knees.

He takes the hint and lets himself out, while the engines still running, I fold myself in half, to exit as quickly as possible behind him. As I reach to pick up Mickey, I see a figure in a white dressing gown pass, ten metres from the car. It's Dad. I'm positive it's Dad. Most likely sneaking out for a crafty cigarette before the doctors give him a lecture on his lifestyle, with Mickey out of the car, I look up again, he's still there, walking without a care in the world. I make to follow him, Mickey on my hip, and as I near him, he smiles, that huge ear-to-ear smile, he places a finger to his lips, and winks. I'm almost close enough to whisper, "Why?" When Uncle Peter drags me back. I turn with a scowl.

"What?" I ask. I'm annoyed he's interrupted this moment.

"You're going the wrong way, your mum's waiting for you."

"She's fine." I snap, and turn to give Dad a, "mother's families always been a bit crackers", look, but he's gone. It's quiet and dark, Mickey looks scared. I concede, and follow where Uncle Peter's leading me, concluding Dad would meet back there anyhow. He'd never leave mum, not for any length of time. Come to think of it, why weren't they smoking together?

I didn't have long to wait for the answer, lightly dragged to the relatives room, I see Aunty Sara already there. There's a man I don't recognise, and my mum in the centre of the pair. Mum has a half empty box of tissues on her knee, and a face that could just have been slimed. Her eyes are a warning signal red, her hair a sticky mess. Aunty Sara looks at me with fear and trepidation as I walk into the room. All eyes are on me. I feel as if I've just entered the dock at a murder trial. The future uncertain, but most definitely bad.

I don't speak; I don't see the need to. These women, over reacting. Whatever was wrong with Dad must be devastating, yet we still had him. He was still about. Still functioning. Still here. Bright side and all that. Let's look at it.

"He's DEAD. Oh Tinsey I'm so sorry, he's DEAD!"

My, they do over react. I mentally add a few words of my own, making the sentence sound more like, his liver's dead. His left arm is dead. Life before this heart attack is dead.

"We'll survive mum, don't worry, couple of months, we'll get through this."

I truly imagined a problem that could be fixed. Dad needing to give up smoking, to exercise more, maybe taking a bit of care of.

"Couple of months? Are you delusional, your father is dead?"

The words begin to sink in. Drop by drop they permeate. How?

"How?"

Mum just shakes her head, cries some more. Aunty Sara looks to me, "they couldn't revive him, they tried, but it was too late. He had a blood clot. He couldn't be saved."

"I've just seen him, outside."

"No, Tinsey, it can't be him. He's in the resuscitation room."

Mum looks up through wet eyelashes.

"Do you want to see him?"

"See him? What do you mean?"

"See his body. Do you want to see his dead body?"

This feels like a knife wound straight through my lungs. The air escapes, I fight to reclaim some oxygen from the room. I have just seen him, walking about. Why on earth would I like to see him inanimate, post pain, dead?

"How could you ask me that? Of course I don't. I want to see him alive!"

Mum returns to the tissues. I can't cry. Only stare. I don't want to believe.

I take Mickey for a walk outside, and to have a cigarette of my own, many cars pull up. Mum's brother Paul, his daughters, Grandad.

Grandad walks to me first, Mickey is playing by my feet, whinging a little for ice cream. One of uncle Pauls daughters scoop him up, start tickling him. I'm grateful, but I don't smile.

Grandad is short, shorter than I am, and I'm only five foot two and a peanut. His big blue eyes look up at me, his leathery wrinkled friendly face, wide open. He doesn't ask the question, but I know he's waiting.

"He's dead." I mutter. I forget he's hard of hearing.

"Who's what?"

"Dad, my dad."

"What about him. Where is he, where's your mother?"

"In there, Dad's dead."

"By your Dad's bed?"

"He's DEAD!"

It sounds so cold, so unemotional, so clinical, so detached, and as I turn around, mum is standing behind me, the mystery man holding her elbow.

"I think its best you wear kid gloves for the time being. You're mother has suffered a devastating loss."

I nod. Because, I haven't lost anything. I don't feel as if I've lost anything. I don't have pieces missing. Dad's here, he's with me. Nothing they can say will take that away.

While the family rush forward to comfort mum, they ignore Mickey and I. We use the opportunity to find a vending machine. Mickey, satisfied, on my hip, sucking a rare treat of a dairy milk bar, I take him for a scan of the hospital's perimeter.

I must find Dad again. I must. He's the only one I'd accept comfort from right now. He'd sit on the kerb with me; tell me a story of his own life that would relate to how I'm feeling at this moment. He'd make sense of all the anguish, and most of all, make me feel safe. With Dad in control, we could relax, lay back, enjoy the ride, yet three hours without him, with every step I felt Mickey and I were about to fall off the end of the earth. I had to find him.

I stop close to the ambulance dock. Coming to rest on a bench where we can observe all activity, yet still be at a safe distance to avoid interaction. Mickey tries to force the chocolate bar into my mouth, he knows chocolate helps on a sad day, yet today, it makes me want to vomit, again. I pat his head, and whisper in his ear. Oblivious to the cold myself, I take Mickey's bare feet in my hands and rub them. He seems content enough.

I think of how Dad would handle this, what he would say. If he would say anything. His own father died three months ago. I was with Dad when he took the call.

His face turned white whilst he received the news from his brother, my uncle Bobby, over the phone, yet his voice betrayed nothing.

Dad was the youngest of four. Londoners through and through. Dad adored his mum, and grew up despising his father's violent temper. In a bid to protect his mother and older sister from his father's violent rages, Dad had often fought his father, his father, unsurprisingly won against a child most times, and found Dad too much of a liability. When Dad was five minutes late home one evening, his own father deadlocked the door. Leaving Dad homeless on the streets of London. He was twelve years old.

It took years before they spoke again. Always a volatile relationship. Many fallings out, yet in Dad's strong state of mind, it seemed the only reason dad kept the thread of this fragile family together, was for approval. A reason for it all, for answers, for acceptance. To see glimmers of good, to hope, to dream his father was a better person. Unfortunately, it takes more than beatings, abuse, and ridicule to break a father son bond.

Dad put the phone down, flicked the kettle on, and then sat opposite me at the kitchen table. He wrung a tea towel between his hands whilst staring into the distance.

"That was your uncle Bobby."

We only heard from Uncle Bobby at New Year. A drunken phone call at 1 am, never failed. I adored him nonetheless. It was exciting to hear from him. It had been seventeen years, yet he could still be ringing to visit.

"Is he coming up?"

Dad shakes his head, looks at his hands working overtime.

"My dad, he rang to say my dad's dead. "

I didn't rush forward to hug him. I could have done, yet, not being a tactile family, this would have only added to the discomfort.

"Aw Dad, bloody hell, I'm sorry. I really am."

"He died at Oxford circus tube station. He didn't have his ID on him. He'd left on the Sunday morning for a car boot. Just him, a wad of cash, and an umbrella. It wasn't until Bobby started phoning round, trying to find him. It took your uncle Bobby three days to find him, had to see countless dead bodies first. Three days? He died alone, on the platform, waiting for the green line. Nobody called an ambulance until they were certain it was real, the heart attack. Gosh I hated the evil old bastard, but he didn't deserve that, surely?"

"No, no he didn't dad. At least at eighty-two, he could still take himself off to a car boot? He did quite well really."

"I better ring Phyllis." Phyllis was the long-suffering second wife. Dad's mum died as I was born. My mum wanted me to be named after her, her parting words were, "please don't name her after me, I won't rest easy thinking I may impart even a little of my life on her."

She suffered a terrible life with Dad's dad, violence, abuse, her children being her only comfort. Phyllis fell for the charm of a widow, it took precisely eight months before she took off were my Grandma had left. Financially and emotionally tied, she'd most probably prayed for this day.

"Will you go to the funeral Dad?" A loaded question, yet the answer was instant.

"No. Definitely not. Why? To be a hypocrite? To have the others think I've crawled out of the woodwork at the sniff of a will? Nah, nah, I won't be going."

"Are you ok Dad, how do you feel?"

"That's just it. I don't. I just feel numb."

Praise is for tiny miracles, because if Dad was feeling one drop that day of what I am suffering right now, then I failed miserably in my duty of loving daughter.

Chapter 4

Somehow, in a strange daze, the relatives find Mickey and I and they bundle us into a car to take us home. Mum and dad's house.

As we all wait in the dark for mum to turn the key in the lock, she turns to me,

"I can't go in here if I have to think I'll be on my own. Promise me you'll move in, you'll come stay with me, please."

In my grief, I can only mutter, "of course." I see no reason why not. Mickey and I are alone too. There is no one waiting for us at home either.

The group rub me on the shoulder, call me a good girl, and that's all I receive for my loss. The full amount. That's it. I realise with a jolt, I'm quite simply not expected to grieve, and in trying to do so, I'm actually coming across quite selfish. At least I know the etiquette now.

We walk through the porch into the living room. Mum and dad had only moved into the country railway cottage three months before, their attempt at an early retirement, to enjoy the grandchildren, to exit the rat race. The cottage, as if symbolising this, is bare. No central heating, very little double-glazing. The traffic is quite loud outside and the intermittent trains shake the foundations with a roar. The carpet is a mass of brown and orange swirls, the staircase, which enters living room, has a banister of rope, nothing else.

There are embers in the brown tiled fireplace, I instinctively kneel down to poke the ash, to try to find a flame. Since childhood, we'd always had a real fire, my parents never tempted by a gas or electric substitute. My aunty Sara takes Mickey, and tries to settle him on the sofa behind me. Mum mutters something about putting him in her bed, and I return to the fire. I stare at the glowing coal, willing it for answers, smiling a little as I think; Dad would have put this coal on the fire. He would have made this. He'd have done his little dance as he shook the coal from the bucket and threw it on, no doubt a couple of pieces escaping, mum berating him for not using the tongs. Dad just smiling, hearing it a thousand times before.

The conservatory leads left from the sitting room, and through its double glass doors, I catch a glimpse of white. Someone walking past the windows, I try to see it again, but my Uncle Paul breaks my concentration.

"Let me get this fire going, think we should start again. Pass me that lighter."

I look to my right and see my dad's tobacco tin, brass with a tiny gold eagle on the top right corner, his disposable lighter resting beside it.

"No."

He shakes his head at me and leans forward for them regardless.

I take them first, "I said, no. These are dads. I want them here. Right here, just where he left them."

He shrugs and wanders to the kitchen, the whispers begin, and I have a feeling they're not going to stop for some time. I couldn't care less. Dad only met the man a handful of times. Why on earth he should be here in this most private time is beyond me, and to add insult to injury, he's brought his children. Children I'm expected to amuse. On any other day, I'd have been pleased to see them. Today though I don't have the capacity to think about anyone else but myself. It may be selfish, it may be rude, it may be self-obsessed, all I know is, I'm not deliberately acting this way. It is as if part of my mind has shut down, my processing ability gone, the blinkers are on, and I can only see a second ahead and just how I'm going to pull myself through that second, and onto the next. Never before have I understood just how much time travel would mean to grieving people. A couple of hours, that's all. That's all I'd need. I begin my fantasy, and shut the rest of the world out.

I'm left alone for an hour, when I hear Mickey cry. It pierces my consciousness. I rise slowly, take the steps up to where he lay in bed and as I do, the front door opens. With a gust of fresh air, and a silence in the constant hum of chatter, my aunty Stephanie and two of her daughters arrive. They see me on the stairs, say nothing, and run forward to hug my mum. I carry on, hardly breaking step, I find Mickey in my parents bed, and curl in beside him.

My eyes are wet; I don't want Mickey to see them. He settles with me there, starts tugging my hair; I turn my back to him, and see the bedside table.

Dad's book, page turned down at the corner, only half read. Like an electric bolt, it hits me; he'll never read the rest, he'll never know the end. Ever.

I'll never be able to moan to him about my mother's family. How they ignore me because I'm half southern and ambitious, how I dare to dream beyond the North. Mickey will never have another grandad; I'll never have my dad. Fatherless, both of us. I cry.

Huge racking, body wrenching sobs. For myself and my loss, I cry. No thought makes me feel better. Ingrained in me, has been the ability to put a positive spin on any situation, yet, there can be none with this. There is nothing good about any of this, and there is no reason for this to end. Unless dad walks into the room right now, this pain, this physical and mental anguish, won't end.

So I cry. Mickey cries. Nobody comes to us, nobody comforts us, and at some point we must have fallen asleep, clinging to each other as survivors of the Titanic would to a lifeboat.

It's Aunty Sara who wakes me up.

"Teenz, Teenz, come on, your brother will be here soon. He's on his way, come on."

I look at her through the slits which are my peepholes, I squint, I feel my head bang, will it not to be yet another migraine starting, for a second I forget why I'm here, wonder why dear Luke is gracing us with the presence of his gold plated balls, and then it hits, and I ask, quite nastily,

"Why the hell did you wake me up? I was sleeping. I could forget while I slept. Why wake me up? WHY?"

Aunty Stephanie must have heard me shout as she comes into the bedroom now. Her huge matronly frame, and no nonsense attitude, not scary today.

"Your mother needs you up. There's a lot to organise. Your mother's in no state to do it. It falls to you. It's your responsibility. I have to go home to my husband now, so get up and go and look after your mother, there's a good girl, come on."

Aunty Sara shrugs, "I'm taking Uncle Peter home, then I'll be back, if you want me to stay the week I will, I'll help, I promise."

I squeak my reply, "please."

I see Mickey is already downstairs. He's sat on the sofa, a piece of toast in his chubby hands. My mum is slouched in dad's chair. The chair had been leased out for the set of a popular TV series that was filmed in my dad's last antique shop, huge, comfortable, yet stately at the same time. It has carved oak handles in the image of dragon heads, royal green cord with a brass studded trim and an ornate carved frame. Coincidentally, the part it played was to hold an actress as she collapsed from a heart attack. A flash of dad comes to me, animate, excited, telling me how they stood back whilst the director ordered her to be more breathless, more wobbly, less well. Unbeknown to my father, he was actually watching a scene of how he was going to die, on the very same chair. This may or may not have been fate. I have absolutely no doubt that it was the same force, preparing my father, as it had me only last week. Adjusting his mind, so he would accept the fate when his time came.

With connections such as these, a lifetime of superstition ingrained into my moral conscience, I'd usually demand the chair were sold, that it must hold bad karma or bad luck, however, I didn't feel it with this. It was a comfort to see it. To concentrate and see Dad, smoking roll ups with a huge mug of tea next to him, either doodling on the Times, talking on the phone, fiddling with small antiques, or peering out of the window with binoculars determined to find the huge Black Panther that was fabled to be stalking the North Yorkshire Moors. This chair was going nowhere.

I sit next to Mickey and mum looks at me with red eyes. We don't talk.

I hear laughter from the kitchen, and I'm amazed how. How can people be laughing? How can they even muster a smile? Don't they understand, the world has ended, it has stopped turning. Nothing will ever be the same again. Our futures wiped out in an instant, don't they see that? How can they be so cruel? Mum whispers, barely audible, I ask her to repeat it.

"Don't judge them Tinsey, it's the only way they know, he wasn't their husband, or father after all."

Aunty Sara, hearing mum speak, breezes into the living room, her whole aura a sea of nervousness, walking on eggshells, she's holding a cup of tea. She holds it out towards me, I take it to warm my hands, nothing more. I am a coffee drinker in a morning, this doesn't matter right now though, nothing could be more insignificant.

As Mickey wipes a buttery hand down my jeans I realise I'm still in yesterdays clothes and so is he. We have nothing here, our house is only a two minute drive away so I try to organise a mini rota in my head for picking up clothes, nappies, food, yet a black tar enters my brain, and I feel as if I'm wading through setting concrete.

The tears threaten to start again, I can't have Mickey or mum seeing me, I have to be strong. I'm really trying.

Aunty Sara sits next to me, and talks in a loud whisper, I'm sure she thinks mum can't hear, yet she's only two feet away, and hasn't lost her marbles yet, just her life.

"You need some things. Danny and Anna are coming; they'll take you to your house. Pick up what you need, you'll be here for a while. You don't have to do anything else today. Tomorrow, I'll need to talk to you, there's a lot to do tomorrow, but forget about that now, Luke's coming in an hour."

Aunty Steph, at the mention of golden nuts, demands attention from the entire room, while she enters, ripping half a slice of toast from her mouth.

"Yes, Luke will sort everything out. He'll take charge. He'll do it. Everything will be ok as soon as Luke's here."

"Woo Hoo," I mutter.

I want to scream at her, so golden nuts is going to bring my dad back is he? IS HE? Because apart from that, I cannot see how everything could possibly be OK!

I don't though. This is just as well as she's leaving. She has a fake smile on her face and a patronising tone, when she bends down to kiss my mother on the cheek.

"You're not the only one that's grieving Sylvia, we miss him too."

I see the look in mum's eyes, the incredulous disbelief, as it is mirrored in my own. This woman who only saw my father at Weddings and special occasions, who has never had more than a five minute conversation with him, is comparing her grief, taking our grief, and expecting us to have sympathy for her, at a time when neither of us can even organise our minds enough to make a simple instant coffee?

Mum shakes her head, takes a tissue, and lowers her eyes again. Aunty Steph straightens herself to leave. She passes Aunty Sara on the way to the front door. Aunty Sara has Mickey on her hip now, she's wiping his face.

"Ring the doctor again, see if he can't give her some Valium, it's awful seeing her like this."

Aunty Sara shrugs, "I tried because I've got to leave them for the day today, but the doctor said she has to grieve, it's a natural process, she has to do it."

"Fair enough, get her a bottle of brandy then, I've put a bit in her tea. I've got to get back to my own family," she raises her own voice a little louder, "so I'll see you all at the funeral, yeah?"

Mum nods, I sip my tea, Aunty Sara walks her to the door. They're almost there when Aunty Steph pops her head around the porch; she looks straight at my mum.

"You'll need Mike's van moving for the funeral, not everyone will get in the drive, and I know you or Tinsey won't be driving it."

Mum shrugs, "whatever."

"Well, it's brand new, shame to see it rot; my Ronnie's always wanted a van like that."

"He can have it."

Aunty Sara shakes me a little, as if some of this should be sinking in, as if I should be saying something.

"Look we'll make decisions in a few weeks, Luke might want it. Wait until Luke gets here." I say.

Aunty Steph's angry, "tell you what, I'll ring you Sylvie, better we talk without interruptions, I'll ring you."

I let it pass, but store it to memory, wondering, how in such a tragic situation human nature could make vultures out of family.

Chapter 5

All hail sir Golden Nuts! For thou has entered thine palace, to take control, to right all wrongs, to fill thine house with manliness.

Like lolloping excited puppies, the people in the house rush outside as soon as Luke's taxi pulls up. Anna had arrived on her mother's departure, Danny with her. Aunty Sara's kids, they are my cousins. I attended primary school with Danny, Anna is Luke's age. Aunty Sara has dropped Mickey off at private nursery on her way home. Luke exits the car with a nodding of his head, his gorgeous glamour puss wife closely behind. Anna holds her brother back with an extended arm, so mum can pass on the path and reach him. As she does, she crumples in his arms. I hold back, observing from a distance, and as the tears fall from Luke's face, I can't tell who is holding who up.

Through my grieving fog, the one I'd become quite used to, I hear my name,

"Tina," then sobs, "Tina, where is she? Where's my little sis?"

Almost frantic. Anna pushes me forward to greet the prodigal son, and he scoops me into his wide embrace, and holds on so fiercely it almost stings. For the second time is as many hours, I find myself wishing I was stronger. Wishing I could take the whole of the pain away, for now, though, I am grateful for his presence. My earlier thoughts unjustified, he's united mum and I in our grief.

He lets go of me, pats me on the head, and walks mum into the house. She's talking more than I've heard her talk in the last twenty-four hours. He's brought a little of her back to life, and that can only be a good thing. Anna and Danny hold back too, seeing their need for a little privacy. Luke's wife, Helen, is stood talking in hushed whispers to Anna; Danny joins me on an unsteady bench on the path.

"How you're doing Teenz, how ya holding up?"

I look at my cousin, his boy band looks, I missed him growing into this man. So close at primary age, as soon as our hormones kicked in, we grew apart. He is married now and has a little girl. He's the first one since Dad's death to ask me how I am.

"Not good." I can't construct a longer sentence.

"Nobody thinks of the children, you know. I didn't believe Mattie, but just looking now, he's right."

"Mattie?"

"Matt Oggy, you remember, fat little kid? Well he's 24 now. He lost his dad last year, Tom."

"Of course," and I nod, Tom was the life and soul of many a wedding or christening. His wife Sue and himself are best friends with Aunty Sara and Uncle Paul. He'd been diagnosed with cancer after he complained of stomach ache. He died a month later.

"Well, Mattie said to me at the funeral, he said it was as if he didn't exist. As if the only one who had lost someone was his mum. No one ever asked how he was, or gave him any sympathy, just kept telling him to be strong for Sue."

"Some one must have helped him through."

"No, no one. So I'm saying now, at the funeral, don't expect it. Everyone will comfort your mum; you're supposed to just cope."

"I don't think I can Danny, I really don't."

"Bloody hell Tinsey, if you can't there's no frigging hope for the rest of us. Your dad was the strongest person I know, and you're the next. You take after him Tinsey; we always talk about how strong you are. You dumped a blinking rock star, whilst you were pregnant for heaven's sake. That takes some doing."

"I always had my dad behind me Danny, with him there, I could handle anything."

"You'll find it without him, somehow, you will."

I nod and start biting my nails. Looking across to the North Yorkshire moors, I can feel the chill in the air, although it hasn't been announced, the air felt of autumn. Of cinder toffee and hot chestnuts, fallen leaves, and the great Hull fair. Dad and I were planning to take Mickey this year. Danny has thoughts of his own, he starts chuckling.

"I absolutely adored Uncle Mike," he says.

"I know you did, everyone did. I still do."

"I remember when I was about 8, your dad had the antique shop at the top of our road, Spring Bank, I found a grotty fake metal ring in a gutter. So I took it to your dad, to sell. I'd seen him buy tonnes of gold and silver. He knew I'd been in and out of the newsagents next door, eyeing up a light up yo-yo, but I didn't have the money for it.

"He umm'd and ahh'd, I knew it was rubbish, it may even have been a ring pull off a can of coke, without the dirt on it, but your dad pretended it was something special.

"Tell you what Dan," he said, "If I clean this up, make it shine, I could make a pretty penny on this son. How much do you want for it?"

I didn't know what to say, because I knew in my heart it was rubbish, so I didn't dare to.

"Tell you what," said your dad, "nip in next door, get me a packet of rizlas, yourself that new yo-yo in the window, and we'll call it quits, whatcha think?"

"I jumped up and down, I was so happy, I really was. I've never forgotten that, never."

I smile through the tears. Danny is doing the same.

"I loved that shop, the white phone box next to it, Dad took the door off, so he could hear the phone ring. He even had his cards printed up with the public telephone's number!"

Danny laughs, "Yeah we used to go pester him after school, and he'd get us making pictures, or varnishing, polishing brass by the fire. Instant tea!"

"Yeah, bloody instant Tea with milk in. Do they still make that?"

"No idea."

Our reminiscing is interrupted by Anna, breezing past jangling car keys, Luke's wife Helen closely behind.

"Come on Tince," she orders, "let's leave Luke and your mum alone, you need some stuff if you're going to be living here now."

She's right, I want to be with Luke and Mum, to be with the ones who have lost, yet I haven't the energy to argue, and it would be nice to have some clean pyjamas for Mickey for tonight. Living though? I don't want to live here.

I let it pass. Helen keeps her own council, but I can see her reading my mind.

As we enter my house through my bookshop, it feels cold. Draughty, empty, unloved. I want to light the fires, rearrange the books, curl up with Mickey on one of our cosy sofas, and stare at nothing. I want to be home. Obligation forces me forward. I don't seem to know why I'm here, or what I'm doing, so I put myself through the motions. I walk from room to room touching nothing. Both Helen and Anna plonk their bums on said comfy sofas, pull their coats around them, and shout to me. Their breath visible in the cold air. The house has central heating but is a breezy old place, characteristic. It's ours.

I throw items into a bin bag, empty a couple of drawers, pack some favourite snacks of Mickey's, his blanket, a few toys, then I can't think of anything else, so I stop. I stand in front of the empty fire as if an imaginary flame is warming my behind. I am exhausted. Just five minutes of concentration and physical exertion, and my body can't take it. My head feels too heavy for my neck, my shoulders ready to slump. I ache from top to toe, and my mind is fuzzy.

Anna must see something in me, as she proffers half a Twix.

"You need to eat, you can't stop eating."

I take it, but retch with the first bite. It's not that I've stopped eating, it's how am I ever going to start again? How can I eat for pleasure, when my Dad is lying cold and alone in a hospital mortuary? It's impossible. Anna seems to understand.

"It's nothing to do with your dad. It's your mum, your mum needs you, if you don't eat, who will take care of her, and Mickey? You have to eat, you have no choice."

Helen speaks up; I've not even uttered a word.

"Look, I know it's hard, Luke and I will help you this week, but after that, we're gone, back to London, then it's just you. It can't be helped."

I nod, swallow the rest of the chocolate almost whole, it hurts, and tastes alien, disgusting, and I wonder if I up my sugar intake in coffee, maybe I won't have to eat again for a little while. The thought comforts me as we return to the house.

Helen and I are dropped off by Anna about a hundred yards from the house, she's rushing, she's done her bit, and now needs to be home with her own family. We're walking in silence alongside the grassy banks when we find an injured kestrel at the side of the road. It's wide-awake and obviously alive, yet one wing is splayed and broken, the other wrapped tightly around its body. Golden feathers, with brown specks and mesmerising yellow eyes make him a creature to revere. I tell Helen we have to save him, so she picks up her pace, walking purposely, muttering about Golden Nuts. Saying Luke would know exactly what to do. Luke who has only ever lived in a city? I sigh, and follow, a few paces behind.

Three minutes later, I'm still walking back, when they pass me with an empty cardboard box and a towel. I leave the pet rescuers to it, and enter the house with a little trepidation, as mum is alone. I don't know what to say to her. She's sat in Dad's chair. She tries to smile at me, but fails. I sit on the floor and await the kestrel's delivery. I'm shattered; staring at the front door is all I can do. All I want to do.

They barge in within seconds; show the bird to my mum, who rings her friend. They discover an animal rescue centre is less than two miles away, and arrange to drop it off.

"You coming sis?" Asks Luke, he means well, I can think of nothing worse. Conversing with strangers when my eyes won't stop leaking, they'll think I'm batty. I don't need strangers right now, and I don't want to be a gooseberry between Luke and his wife. As lovely as they are, they tend to forget I'm there, whisper and kiss, and basically embarrass me. So no.

"No, I'll stay here with mum." I'm thinking it may be nice to have five minutes alone with mum. I still need her. I still need my mum. She's all I've got to comfort me. She's the only one who understands.

"Go with them!" mum orders, from nowhere.

"I don't want to," I answer, tears threatening to prick again.

She shrugs and they leave.

I look to her for comfort, for empathy, for a mutual understanding of why leaving the house once is enough, instead mum snarls at me.

"You need to pull yourself together, for pity's sake!"

"I just didn't want to go. I didn't want to see strangers."

"You have a three year old child! You don't have time to think about what YOU want!"

"I best go get him then." I walk quickly from the house. The tears falling like heavy rain down my face, turning the ignition through a blur of salt water, I plead with Dad, all the way to the nursery.

"WHY? WHY? I miss you so MUCH. I need you Dad. PLEASE! I love you. Dad, PLEASE, I can't do this. HELP me!! "

My voice horse, my eyes barely slits, by the time I pull up in the car park, yet it's not until darkness falls, that Dad answers my plea for help.

Chapter 6

As I enter the house with Mickey, Luke, Helen, Aunty Sara and mum are sat around talking. It stops as we walk in. I busy myself unpacking, whilst running Mickey a bath. Luke flicks on the TV, and tries to find a channel with sport on it. Helen picks up a newspaper, Aunty Sara follows me into the kitchen, the bathroom's downstairs.

"I've made some appointments for tomorrow, it has to be done. I've the funeral director coming at three, and then you need to register your dad's death at four. Pick Mickey up on your way home."

I nod, it's not sunk in, but I nod. The bath run, I undress Mickey, ruffling his hair, trying to play the part, even though I feel nothing. He splashes in the few inches of water as I sit on the loo seat, the door slightly ajar.

Suddenly, he's giggling, and uncontrollable giggle. Like someone's tickling his belly, or pulling faces at him. I look at him, and see him staring straight at the door, a finger to his lips as he giggles.

He splashes louder, his feet up and down, making mini waves.

"GAN DAD, GAN DAD!" My tears start again. Mickey can't see me at all.

"K shhhhh....." He's still talking to the door. He whispers now, as if someone has asked him to be quiet.

"Gan dad." He's so happy. There's nothing there.

Aunty Sara has made bacon sandwiches; Mickey eats his sat on my lap in the living room. He puts his plate down, walks to mum, and pushes her back in her chair, "lay down." He says, and toddles back to his food.

We watch television together without seeing anything, and as I take Mickey upstairs to what will become our room, I bid goodnight to all at the same time. I can't bear to spend another moment in silence surrounded by people. I can't worry about their feelings, I can just manage to focus on Mickey, anyone else, forget it. We lay on the oak double bed, Mickey cuddles into me, reaches an arm round tugs at my ear. He's exhausted, his rosy cheeks rising and falling as he drifts into a heavy sleep.

"Gan dad," he whispers, as I feel my own eyes beginning to close.

"Gan dad gone," I murmur, pulling him closer.

"Gan dad here mummy. Gan dad here." As I fall asleep, Mickey begins to gently snore and still aware of the TV and hushed voices downstairs, I see Dad.

It seems as though through my eyelashes, yet there's a swirl of colours, a corkscrew that widens at the top. Like a tornado, only prettier. We're stood before some doors, huge arched mahogany doors with cast iron fixing and hinges, they look old, but I know without trying that they will open with ease, we're stood on worn limestone steps. They are very plain, nothing fancy. Dad has his favourite leather flying jacket on, grey trousers, tee shirt. He looks as he did any other day.

I run forward to hug him. He holds me close; the hug feels like everything good compounded into a squeeze, every happy moment I've cried at, every good exam result, every time I'd fallen in love or lust, the birth of Mickey, winning a relay race, waking up as a child on a Christmas morning, everything. The hug is almost overpowering how good it feels, it fills me with a warm light and I just know, it's taken away all of the pain, this is real, this is everything, this is new, and I don't want to let go.

Without opening his mouth, Dad speaks to me. I can hear him, yet he's not making a sound.

"Come on, you silly Bugger," he's saying, " come on, that's enough, you don't need to cling on. You'll be fine."

I speak, I do make a sound, and I do open my mouth, "you're back dad, you're back!"

He looks forlorn. I didn't expect that. I expected joy. "For you Tince, for now, just here, I'm back, I'll always be here whether you see me or not, but for everyone else, no. They have to move on."

"But it's easy dad, just come with me, just, please, make the steps." I go to open one of the double doors, I feel if dad will walk with me, come with me through the doors, he'll be back for good.

"I can't," he shakes his head and looks at the floor. I feel like I have the emotional, physical and mental strength of ten men since our hug, however, Dad seems lost. As if, he has to leave but doesn't want to. As if going away to work for months.

"I've got to tell them you're back Dad."

"Go through the doors, Tince, I can't go through there, not anymore. You go, leave me. That's where you should be. I'll be here for you, just not for a little while."

I refuse to move. I don't want to leave him. He knows this and starts walking away. As if obligation is pulling him. Or the greater good, I can tell he doesn't want to go, but is being strong for me.

"As long as you're here Dad, I'll cope, I promise. Don't worry about me, please don't worry."

"Good, go. See you in a minute."

"I love you Dad."

"You daft sod, just go, go on."

I open the door to daylight filling a hall. Chairs lined in rows. Mum's friend Jane meets me; I turn around to point out dad to her,

"Dad's back, he's back, Dad's back…." as I point the door swings shut, then disappears altogether. Julie holds my hands in hers.

"He's back for you, you won't see him though, we won't see him. He can never be back the way you'd like. You're probably best not telling anyone else, they'll think you're potty, they think I am."

With that the room we're in fills with daylight, blinding, I open my eyes, and realise; I'd not closed the curtains the night before. Mickey is waking beside me, I feel my pillow, and this time it's dry. I'd not cried through the night, and right now, I feel ok. Not fantastic, still sad, still as if I've lost a huge part of me, but bearable. I know what I must do, and I know to make Dad happy I must be strong; I must try to take control and ease the burden. I must try.

First stop, funeral. I skip down the stairs with a renewed energy, I find Aunty Sara in the kitchen, making toast. Luke is eating some, reading a paper, mums still in the chair, and it sounds as if Helen is in the bath.

"We're going to have this and then go for a walk; do you want us to take Mickey?" Asks Aunty Sara, without even turning round.

"Who's going?" I ask.

Just me, and Helen, the priests coming, we thought it would be best if just you, Luke and your mum saw him for the first time."

I nod, this is good. "Yeah, yeah, ok, please. Another thing."

"Go on."

"I don't want to miss the funeral director this afternoon; I need to be here for him. I don't know why, I just know I do."

"That's fine, but you've to register the death at 4. Only you can do it, it has to be a relative. Your mum's not up to it."

This may seem a little confusing; of course Luke is here, Golden Nuts. Golden Nuts was born to a rich Canadian Forester two years before mum and dad even clapped eyes on each other. Mum had married Luke's father, but like many marriages, it didn't work out, lucky for me. I wouldn't be here if it had.

Mum and Dad fell in love quickly. Mum worked behind the bar in a nearby town, Dad had taken on a contract in the North. Away from his surroundings, with the voice of Adam Faith, and the looks of a young Ray Winston he was soon in demand by the ladies. All accept one. My Mum. With a two year old boy at home, the last thing mum needed was a cockney wide boy complicating her life; it took dad two months of charm before they finally took a stroll together along the beach.

Dad left soon after that, his business taking him back down south, and mum despite herself, found herself longing for any form of correspondence from him. When the first postcard arrived with a sunset sprawled across the front, mum jumped for joy, and they became pen pals for quite a while, until mum wrote about her worries for her house. Since the divorce, she could no longer keep up payments on the house, or of the furniture in it. After receiving mum's letter, dad hopped on a train with a suitcase, turned up at mum's door, and opened the suitcase, to reveal tonnes of bottles of the best brandy money can buy. It wasn't a solution, but it sure helped mum to greet the bailiffs with a smile! From then on, they became inseparable despite their obstacles.

Mum's family in particular, my grandfather, aunties, including Aunty Stephanie was completely against a southerner. The north South divide evident even as Britain moved itself into the eighties, pushed by Maggie Thatcher. It took twenty years for them to accept him fully, and then, only a few years later we are here discussing his funeral. Today I pitied them, because as much as I hate them for not understanding our pain, they will never know what a great person he was. They don't have a clue. Mum and I, and indeed Luke, have been lucky, we've had him for a lifetime, almost.

With Helen and Aunty Sally gone, I take my first shower and allow myself to enjoy it. My belly rumbles, and I'm suddenly ravenous. Once clean and dry, I pinch a jumper of Dads, his socks, and some leggings of mums. No makeup. I'm cosy and awake, that's enough. I take Dad's butcher style pork scratching's from the cupboard and sit to eat them as Luke lets the priest in. Mum looks at me as Luke chats in the porch.

"You think I was horrible yesterday, don't you?"

I consider lying, but realise it would serve no purpose now. Little I could say could open mum's wounds any further, the truth wouldn't even touch it.

"Yes, yes I do. But I get it. I know why."

"I was just scared, for Mickey that's all. Me, I'm in no state to look after him, but seeing you crumble, I couldn't handle that."

"Fair enough, I'm here now, I know what I've got to do. We know dad, we love him, so only us should arrange his final days. Yeah?"

Mum nods. She's agreeing. She understands.

"But mum, please, please don't give anything of his away, not yet, eh? Please."

"Tinsey, take what you want, anything."

"I've got all I want mum, for now, but later, as Mickey grows older, as you reminisce, who knows, so hold on yeah?"

The priest enters, and puts a stop to our conversation. He's wearing a huge sympathetic smile, a brightly coloured jumper; he immediately puts us at ease. He has a guitar slung over his shoulder, with a rainbow strap.

As he sits as close to mum as he can, holding one of her hands in his, I chew on particularly large pork scratching.

"Do you have to have those for breakfast?" Luke scolds, "Could you not pick something a little quieter, sounds like you have hollow cheeks."

I don't answer as I've a mouth full. Mum does instead.

"Leave her be Luke, I don't care how much noise it makes, as long as she eats, ok?"

"With her hollow cheeks, there's an echo though, it's so annoying." He's smiling a touch though. I swallow my pork scratching and reach for another, it's huge.

Luke shakes his head at me as I bring it towards my mouth. I start to giggle.

"Aw mum tell her," laughs Luke, "it's got hairs on it and everything, it's disgusting."

I suck the salt off giggling all the time.

"Tell her mum, make her go in the bathroom and eat them."

Mum's started laughing too, "go on Tinsey, eat it, go on."

I quickly throw it in my mouth and crunch, almost choking through my giggles, Luke shoves his fingers in his ears but is laughing too, we all are. The priest is surveying our hysterics with a look of joy. We stop as we hear the door, Helen, Aunty Sara, and Mickey, home already.

"Tell you what," says Chris the priest, on seeing Mickey, "why don't we", he sweeps an arm, indicating the last people to enter the room, "sing a song, in the conservatory, whilst the immediate family jot down some notes of the best bits of Michael James."

Helen, Aunty Sara, and Mickey dutifully follow Chris the priest as he begins plucking at his guitar, a tune that sounds like, red and yellow and pink and green…. He starts singing, through the glass doors we see Aunty Sara's expression, she mouths, pointing at the back of Chris' head, "I can't believe you've left me with this donut," and we start laughing again.

Chapter 7

The funeral director arrives at three. He is dressed suitably all in black, creeping into the living room after Aunty Sara lets him in, I give him my place on the sofa. He sits diagonally; his knees almost touch mums from her permanent fixture in the chair. Mum has not spent a night upstairs yet, deeming it too painful to contemplate sleeping in their bed alone.

Despite her state mum is obviously still very attractive to this man. He has a glint in his eye that he imagines the new merry widow would polish to perfection. His hands seem like claws, his receding hairline, the same colour as his suit. His mouth is almost wet, and his body language nearly pornographic. I'm kneeled next to Aunty Sara in front of the fire; Mickey is playing with Helen in the conservatory. The funeral director introduces himself as Neil, and begins with the spiel.

He takes mums hand in his and rubs it as he tries to stare into her eyes. I don't think mum can see him, her eyes are so red, unaided by the double shot of brandy in her tea. He starts talking, a barely audible whisper. Designed so mum has to lean in to listen, and the rest of us are left out of the exclusive loop. I instantly despise the man, and I know in my gut, dad would too. His firm though is reputable. I've never been in this situation before, I've no idea if this is common practice or not. I know I don't want him close to my mum though that is a fact.

I move closer myself, and ask him to speak up.

He raises his voice without acknowledging me, directs his words at mum only.

"I know this must be a huge shock loosing Nick like that…"

"Michael," I but in.

"Or Mike," shrugs mum.

"OK" nods Neil. "Losing Mike is the worst thing to happen to you, I understand that, and I'm here to make it easier for you, Nick would want that."

"Michael!" I'm annoyed. He's not endearing himself to me, this funeral director. I want him gone. He lowers his voice again, and whispers to mum, words we can barely hear. Once finished, mum's nodding, so easily influenced by outsiders without my dad's endless wisdom.

"So," he announces, looking straight at me, "we have two times. Monday 9.30am, or this Friday at 4.30pm. The great thing about Friday is, you'll be the last ones, so there'll be no rush."

"Friday." I tell him, without looking at anyone else. They've all agreed with me anyhow. I know taking dad's death into another week will prolong the grieving process whilst interrupting work patterns for the visitors. It's not a great fact of life, but since the dream, I realise, life has to go on here.

Aunty Sara speaks up; she's the most rational of all of us right now.

"So, do you promise there won't be anyone else turning up, no shoeing us out."

Neil nods shuffles some papers, "if you take the Friday slot, yes."

We're all ok with that.

"Next is the venue. The local tavern?" He speeds on. "I can get a spread laid on, and the place booked for a private party for five hundred pounds."

I splutter. "That's ridiculous! We threw mum's surprise 50th there, only cost eighty quid, if everyone's drinking, they're not really bothered."

Neil blusters for a little while, I like seeing him squirm, if he thought for one second I would make this easy on the slimy little creep, he's wrong. He would not be dreaming of coming onto mum, and inflating prices if Dad were here. As fun as Dad was, nobody messed with him. We were safe with Dad around.

"Tell you what," he scowls, "I know the owners, I could maybe talk to them, they'd knock little off."

"A little?" I'm gob smacked.

"Tina..." warns mum. Indicating she wants no unpleasantness. Her eyes say there's enough heartache without adding more.

I shut up, and leave it, quietly seething. I look at the clock; I have five minutes before I'm to set off to the register office. Luke is coming with me. He's been an absolute rock. Sat back, not interfered. Fantastic.

"Ok," Neil continues, he turns away from mum a little, "I know you have to go, so let's just sort the newspaper announcement whilst you're here."

We spend longer than expected discussing how best to word the news of Dad's death, of what we'd like to include, and what we'd like to omit. How soppy or sentimental, the funeral venue details, if we'd like flowers or donations.

"We could make donations to the ambulance service." Neil Suggests.

"NO." Mum and I cry in unison.

The ambulance service took twenty-five minutes to arrive. It took Dad ten minutes to die. Moving him from the house, they dropped him twice, his new white dressing gown falling open. Mum was mortified, angry, and bitter. If they had arrived sooner he may still be alive. We believed this. We also believe that if the doctor had checked his heart, instead of palming him off with indigestion tablets, he'd be alive too. This is the most difficult part to bear, the biggest burden to carry. The what if's. The fact that, despite everything another person was responsible for his death made it all the more unjust. I certainly notice a bitterness, a cynicism creeping in I'd never felt before. Dad has kept us in a bubble, safe from harm, advice on con men, our problems a small chat away from solving, be it financial, physical, and emotional, people, customers, friends, family. Dad had the answers, and when he didn't he knew how to protect us from having to endure the pain.

The most recent example I can give you is this; my first day of running the bookshop was traumatic. The original residents of the town did not welcome outsiders, yet the outsiders did. The shop was popular, yet the grateful shoppers were peppered with the grumpy ones.

I had not envisaged the reaction I would receive as a single mother putting herself in the public eye. A young single mother, with a thin skin, I was a target for bullies. My green gills on display for everyone to see, firstly an advertising company backed me into a corner, I found it impossible to make excuses, no matter how many times I asked, they wouldn't leave. No matter how many times I said no, they persisted. They nagged and nagged, whilst I lost valuable first customers, until eventually I signed on the dotted line, for a direct debit of an extortionate amount to be taken for their services of a small card in a local supermarket. I felt robbed.

Before long, despite the ringing of the till, my second test came. A man, about my age, 23, extremely forward in my empty shop, he leans his lanky body over my counter. Leering at me, asking if I live alone. I can't answer, I don't want him to know that I do, I shake my head, and pick up the phone, pretending to call someone. He starts shouting as he walks out.

"You stupid bitch, you stuck up cow, who the hell do you think you are?" I'm waiting for him to exit, but he turns when he reaches the closed door.

"I only wanted to be your friend? What's so wrong with that?" he kicks a shelf, and a coloured glass ball falls of and breaks, he doesn't notice.

I still have the phone to my ear, I start pressing buttons, the number of dad's mobile. He see this and walks away slowly.

"You can't get rid of me that easily, I won't be brushed off, I want answers!"

I don't care about the answers as he's left, and I can breathe again.

I ring dad whilst sobbing.

"Why are they so horrible, people, why?" I sniff.

Dad laughs but not unkindly, "you need a thicker skin Tinsey. Some people are cruel, but you need to get rid of them, you need to learn how."

"How do I?"

"I've always found a good, 'fuck off' works well." He chuckles. The swearing doesn't bite, as with his London accent it's hardly noticeable.

"I can't say that Dad. Besides, that man today, he was already angry, I've no idea why."

"You didn't give him the answers he wanted; I do think that one had a mental disorder."

"The sales people didn't."

"No, you'll have a lot of them. You need to learn to say no."

"I'll try."

"So, come on, it's your first day, what are your takings today?"

I grin; I love it that he's proud.

"One hundred and ninety three pounds and sixty pence."

"Bloody hell, that's some going, I never knew second hand books would fetch so much money, that's great. So you must have been doing something right then."

"Yeah, now if I could find a way to scare off the horrible ones...."

"Tell you what, in morning, I'll look after the shop for you; you take Mickey on our walk instead."

Mum and Dad had arranged to look after Mickey two days a week to save him being cooped up in the private nursery every day. Dad usually took him for a walk to the sea before taking him home.

I agree and notice the miracle during the following days. The initial cheque I'd written to the advertisers is returned, with an apology for the hard sell. The mental man crosses to the opposite side of the road to pass. Most customers are generally pleasant and respectful, and a few older ladies begin asking when Dad will be managing the shop again.

Dad fixed it for us. No matter what, a tower of strength, he never buckled no matter how heavily we leaned. He'd left me feeling as if I was standing on the peak of Ben Nevis, with no handrail to support me, wobbling, looking, and seeing a long way down. Mortality flashing in neon lights wherever I looked, all possible dangers flooding my brain at the same time as the vertigo makes me nauseous, yet I know, he has shown me well, and I must use his strength as my own now, as he can't use it himself. He may have died, but I still don't want to let him down. Dad would not put up with this poor customer service from Neil, the funeral director.

The slimy toad breaks into my thoughts; I look at my watch and panic. We should have set off ten minutes ago. I stand up, start flustering a little, I want to stay, I don't want to leave mum as prey of this creep, yet, I need to be at the registry office.

"So for the newspaper, we have, Dearest Nick, adored husband to Sylvia, much loved father...."

"No," I interrupt whilst looking for my keys. "It's Michael, how many times, it's Mike or Michael, it was never Nick!" Neil shrugs. He's got his sights set on mum and her widow's pension, I can see it. I see red

Aunty Sara notices me searching for my keys, Luke stands up ready, I can't find them, no pockets, not hand bag, nowhere. I'm becoming angry and stressed, and I have a desire to kick this little weed in the nuts for having so little respect for my father's memory. He's forgotten him, before he's gone with his deliberate slips of the tongue, making him seem less important by the change of a name. A subtle technique that had no doubt worked on a few other widows before, forget the name, focus on the funeral director.

"Take my car," urges Aunty Sara.

"No, no, I want my own for this." I reply rushed. I find my keys in the conservatory with Mickey and Helen, walk back through, Aunty Sara strokes my arm just as Neil leans in to whisper to mum again, it looks almost romantic.

"What's the matter?" asks Aunty Sara, "what's wrong?"

"What's wrong?" I snap, too loudly for comfort, "my father is dead, what else could there be?"

I storm out with Luke following me, once I've calmed down, and let the anger dissipate, I feel like the biggest bitch in the world.

Chapter 8

I've spent the week trying to see Dad, in a physical sense. Although I'd balked at the idea of seeing his dead body initially, now I have a desperate urge to. I miss him so completely I need something, anything to scratch the itch. I imagine seeing him would be the solution.

While Aunty Sara takes care of Mickey, the day before the funeral, mum, Luke and I visit Dad in his place of rest at the funeral home. We had to call first to make an appointment, which has made me a little wary. Dead bodies don't move. Why do we need to call a manned business to ask if they are available? What exactly would Dad be doing? Meeting with the bank manager, finishing touches with solicitor about his will. It seemed little absurd, although I was sure there must be another reason for it.

The receptionist lets us in through the office, it's deathly quiet with a musty smell of lavender and violets. Zoflora disinfectant with a hint of musk I decide. A unique smell and one I won't forget in a hurry. We huddle together in the small office as Neil's business partner, Malcolm, walks through from the back room.

"Would you all like to go together?" He asks. Luke and I are nervous; we've never seen a dead body before. Mum of course saw Dad at the hospital.

We look at each other, and then nod.

"Okay," says Malcolm. "When you're ready, he's in there, straight ahead."

We walk tentatively towards the curtain, each trying to let the other go first, mum takes the lead, Luke grips my hand.

The musky smell is overpowering, I morbidly guess it must be a type of embalming fluid.

"Oh Mike," whispers mum. She leans over a coffin that I can't see the contents of, and kisses something. Luke, the lanky sod, can see and he starts crying silently then he kisses the same place. I have a hand full of pictures and letters from Mickey and I want to put them in the coffin with Dad, but I'm scared to move closer.

"Come on Tinsey, you'll regret it if you don't, you need to say goodbye." Urges mum.

"I'll see him at the funeral." I take a step back. Not quite ready for closure.

"It won't be so intimate then though, they'll be a lot of people saying their goodbyes, you have your chance now, on your own. We can leave if you'd like us too."

"No," I gingerly move forwards, Luke moves gently to a side so I can see. I see Dad's head first, except it doesn't look like Dad, not really.

Luke whispers respectfully, "don't you think he looks so...."

"Pissed off!" I finish.

"Yeah!" Mum and Luke agree in unison.

Dad is crammed into a coffin that seems too small; his expression is one of intolerance, as if the funeral homes staff has grated his nerves with their incompetence. That's the only likeness there is. A passing resemblance to Dad. Without the life in his face, the animation, that we have even when asleep, he just looks like a dead body he could almost be anyone. I feel as if someone has lied to me about the peaceful expression, as I see nothing of the sort. Dad is wearing a black T-shirt and his best grey trousers, mum and I chose the clothes a couple of days before. I reach down, to hold Dad's hand, to lift his arm a little in order to see the tattoo of an Indian girl on his forearm. I needed this identification.

Dad's hand is cold and waxy. Solid, no movement, no pulse. It's grey, not a pink area in sight. Regardless I hold it and raise his arm a little. As I do his fingers close around mine? I'm quite startled but I don't let go.

Mum's shocked, she lets out a squeak, Luke gasps.

I daren't let go, as I am overjoyed with the action, so I shift a little, to make my standing position more comfortable. As Dad's hand lowers, his fingers open, and with disappointment I spot the mechanism of muscles.

"It's a reflex mum, as I pull up a muscle pulls too, which makes his fingers close. It's not Dad."

"No, I know," she sobs, "shame, I thought it was for a minute. Let me hold his hand, I want to feel it all the same."

We swap places, I stroke Dad's forehead, Luke takes the letters and pictures from me, and places them in the coffin. Mum's talking to Dad as if he's still alive; I would, but I feel a little silly, as he's not here. His presence isn't here, there's nothing left. Whatever made Dad himself had left this empty shell already. Taking a better look at him, I see new grey hairs have grown. Within a week, they're quite long, it's odd. I touch them.

"I liked your dad going grey, he was worried about it, but I thought he looked distinguished." Mum uses her free hand to stroke his head.

I have had enough now. There's nothing here, it's stifling, and though I imagined I'd want to spend hours with Dad, I don't. Not like this. Not when he won't even breathe back at me. It seems akin to talking to a tree. Just my opinion, mum obviously has some comfort from it.

I make to leave, tell Dad's body I love him. A tear falls; I wait in the reception for Luke and mum. The smell has permeated my clothes. Not unpleasant, just different, new to me. As I wait, I wonder where Dad is now, and believe more strongly than ever in spirits and all things supernatural.

As the day of the funeral dawns, the flowers arrive first. With only a few moments to choose the adorning chrysanthemums, we were all caught a little off guard. If we were buying for Dad's birthday, Father's Day, and anniversary, we would have been prepared, however, a funeral, although a family get together, is rarely planned for. I know I will regret my choice later, for now however, we have DAD in white, a red rose in each corner.

I've never been to a funeral, but I knew about this arrangement before being shown the book. How lucky I was to always see it on someone else's father's coffin, and not my own. A crying shame, as we never see our fortune at the time. We never appreciate it. Not until the moments, the brief interludes that happen in an instant and change our lives forever. The earth shattering moments that install regret, whilst at the same time shaping us into the person we will ultimately become.

I start the day in a daze, my defences once again shutting down the less important parts of my brain. My mind has filters, as solid as concrete, and nothing lest the most significant messages are pervading. I can see clearly but the world is a blur, fading from one room to the next and back again.

Dad's family arrive first. Dad's older brothers Bobby and Billy, his older sister Nora. I've not seen any of them since I was six years old, neither had Dad. Seeing them all together, squeezed onto the sofa, waiting for a cup of tea I cry.

"Hey," nudges Billy, "don't cry eh? You'll have plenty of time for that after."

"It's wrong," I blub, "it just makes it so clear, that he's missing. That he should be here now. He should be here."

"We have regrets too," says Bobby, "we should have visited more."

I nod, because they should. Then we should have visited them too. Swings and roundabouts.

"Dad was made up to be emailing you, he loved it." Telling people how Dad felt regardless of his input was commonplace this week. Dad had never had his feelings on show as much in his entire life.

There was a lot of truth in this last statement however. Moving to this house to retire meant Dad moved his shop online, and used the outbuildings for storage. His business was doing phenomenally well. After the first hesitations, assuming the computer would bite, I'd spent a lot of time with dad, showing him how to use it, uploading pictures, descriptions, PayPal, escrow, it didn't take long before dad was flying without wings, his business bringing in a small fortune, his expertise appealing to the masses. Another plus of course, the email. Recently, not too long ago, he'd been emailing Auntie Nora and Uncle Bobby, getting to know each other all over again. It was evident at the time, just how happy it made Dad to have his family back in contact. Cruel that his life was taken at this time.

We make polite conversation, I'm comforted by their voices, so similar to Dad's, for a few moments, just letting them talk makes me feel safe again. I feel closer to him than I did staring at his dead body. Uncle Billy pulls a packet of wine gums from his pocket, and my mini euphoric moment is complete. Dad adored wine gums.

Our intimate family gathering is cut short, as strangers and relatives arrive. Mum's enjoying the company, it's giving her less time to think, I can tell; however, she keeps pacing to the conservatory, expecting the arrival of Dad. He's due to arrive any minute. I'd spent last night, polishing and cleaning the room just for him.

Aunty Jacky and Uncle Ade arrive, which is awkward. Jacquie was married to Uncle Bobby over twenty-five years ago; despite having two children together this is the first time they'd clapped eyes on each other since their divorce. Ade, fifteen years younger than Jacky, seemed nervous In Uncle bob's prescience, yet he needn't worry.

Jacky and Ade had been friends of the family for a long time, often visiting for weekends, Uncle Bobbys absence meant this situation had never arose before, however Jacky often commented on the likeness between Bobby and Dad. I see it all too clearly now.

Mum comes to us all, talks in a hush, "the hearse has broken down, with Mike in the back. What shall we do? They don't have another funeral car until this afternoon."

"Use his van." Says uncle Bobby. "I'll drive it."

Mum's a little shocked. Not the answer she was looking for, using a white transit van to move a coffin containing my dead father.

"He'd love it," I chirp in, "proper fools and horse's moment, he'd love it. He'd be laughing at this."

"He did love his van," agrees mum.

"He did, he didn't want all this fuss, he wanted to be buried in a cardboard box." I continue. I like the idea of this. I can hear dad's belly laugh at the thought.

"Ok." Mum's decided.

People laugh as the van arrives, yet instantly the mood shows it's opposite as the coffin is taken from the car. The pallbearers carry dad's coffin through the garden, and like a piece of furniture, have to manoeuvre the six-foot wooden box round the corners of the conservatory doors.

If Dad were stood next to me, we'd both be impersonating the chuckle brothers right now...

"To me - To you- to me - to you- to you - to me."

We'd probably follow this with the Chaz and Dave's, Right Said Fred.

" da de da da de da da…so we take off all the handles…and the things that held the candles….but it did no good, like we never thought it would…..so we have a cup of tea and we thought we ought to…"

Moving furniture was Dad's speciality…an antique dealer it was his trade. I'd been called in to help from as soon as I can remember, although since dropping Dad in it a couple of times, I mostly had to wait in the van until I'd learned the spiel.

Dad did most of his trading between other antique dealers, this little community didn't need customers, a three hundred mile radius, furniture would to and fro, increasing in value with fashion, yet as mum told the priest, Dad was fair, he always charged a little less than he should, leaving a wide margin for the other dealers to benefit from. This not only made him one of the most popular antique dealers of his generation, but also the most respected.

As with most trades, however, there are times, when a little invention means a good sale. A bargain, a find, a gem. A lucky break.

Or an early Victorian washstand sitting pretty on the top of a skip. Dad clocked this as we drove by, I was six. We stopped the car; he put it in the back, with me and a rag. Whilst he drove to a dealer who specialised in this furniture, I dusted it down, made it shine, within ten minutes we were there.

Dad enters the shop, and then exits with Kevin Marshall. Kevin helps dad to take it off the back of the van.

"Nice piece Mike," he admires. "Where's it from?"

"Friend of the wives just picked it up, they want shot."

"How much do they want for it?" Asks Kevin.

"Seventy five quid, but they'd take seventy."

I hear this and think Dad must be mistaken; he's got this piece confused with a few others he has in here, indeed from mum's friend.

"Dad, that one's not seventy quid! How can it be, we just picked it up in a skip for nothing!"

That was that. Wait in the car, speak no evil. I had a lot to learn.

Chapter 9

The coffin is settled on two trestles, making it seem as if it has table legs. The lid is closed. There's dad's chair in the corner, we'd moved it in here on purpose, so people could sit with him, there's also a couple of dining chairs too.

Mums excited for him to be home, almost as if he'd walked through the door himself. In a morbid twist, I can empathise, as I feel quite relieved he's with us, whilst simultaneously trying to broaden my mind to incorporate the coffin.

A coffin is such a symbol, to have one in the house holding one of the most precious people; it's a lot to take in.

Mum stands over the coffin as the pallbearers begin removing the screws for the lid. There's hushed whispers between the guests that have already arrived, especially the younger ones. Dad is no longer a person to them, but a dead body. The normal conversations begin where one asks another if they have ever seen a dead body, if so, where and when. If Dad were alive I'd be fiercely defending him, however, they're right. That's all he is now. A corpse. It should bring comfort, as whatever made him human, whatever made him animated, whatever made him, Michael James, has gone, left this body. Gone to goodness knows where.

Regardless of his soul partying on down in fine old heaven though, this was the last we had of him, much more than a watch, a necklace, the book he was reading, this was the body he wore. We were well within our rights to feel sentimental and for one day only treating it as if he were sleeping.

If it helps us to plod through this devastating day, then so be it.

The lid comes off and clumsily the pallbearers shuffle together, the limited space makes them seem as if they are performing a Greek dance around the coffin lid. The poor young man is discreetly looking for a place to put it, where it won't hinder people traffic. He settles on the garden, it's windy, there's a nip in the air, but it's dry. Luke is stood in the far corner looking out to sea. I join him whilst mum has a semi private moment with Dad.

"Would you look at that," Luke points across to the blue horizon, for the third time this week there's a rainbow.

"I'll always think of Dad when I see a rainbow now." I say. I'm upset but my eyes are dry. I can't cry. I feel as if I should be, but I'm all cried out. They've gone. Late last night I wondered, on a scientific level if my brain has twigged that the tears weren't relieving any hurt, or healing any wounds, so they stopped, an unnecessary side effect, nipped in the bud. The crisp wind makes my eyes sting a little, they water and it feels right.

"I've got to go home tomorrow," says Luke.

"Can't you stay?" I plead. "Just one more week."

"I can't Tinsey; I've got to get back to work. They only gave me a week off. I can't afford to lose my job, my tax bills enormous."

"I know, I know. Just, well what happens now?"

"Get on with life, move forward. Start dating? You could do with a man in your life, you can't live mum's life for her, or her for you, you need your own life."

"I think I'll just concentrate on mum until after Christmas, don't think I could handle a new love right now."

"Just make sure that's all it is. Mum needs you, she does, but you need to make a life for you and Mickey too."

The thought of leaving mum alone fills me with disgust for myself. I know Luke's right, I'll have to do it at some point, I'm hoping when I do, it'll be painless. He sees me pondering on his advice.

"Don't worry about it yet. I get carried away with myself."

I nod my eyes stills stinging. It probably looks as if I'm crying. I'm not.

"Besides, Helen and I will be coming up every weekend to make sure you're all ok, for the first few months at least."

"I just want him back Luke, everything was right with Dad here."

"Of course you do, he was your father. I can't know exactly what you're going through though can I?"

"Why not?" I'm confused.

"Well, my father's still alive and well."

He may as just punched me in the gut, his words wind me. I walk away. I feel too angry and annoyed to stay. Maybe, after a few minutes of calming down I'll understand just how Luke thought I'd benefit from that sentence.

I've never met Luke's dad, have no desire too. Living in Canada, he sounds ok as a person, a coward as a father. He's seen Luke only twice since Luke turned eighteen and was old enough to put himself on a plane. Before that, he'd made no effort to visit him, and whilst living in England had often passed Luke and mum on the street without saying hello. Luke occasionally screeching Daddy, yet still he was oblivious. Wonderful man. Not. So I was biased.

My father gave Luke everything he ever needed, structure, routine, discipline, and his own style of love. Maybe tough at times, but Dad taught Luke how to be a man, to grow up and look after himself, in the playground and on the streets.

Over the past year, with Dad's purchase of the PC, they'd found something in common again, their friendship had cemented into adulthood, instead of the arguments between father and son, a new respect for each other had been found. Dad could often be heard laughing loudly whilst on the phone to Luke. Luke had become Golden Nuts in dad's eyes as well as mums, so proud of his progress and the man he was turning into. It was a joy to see, for mum and me. Luke's defences are up however, and trying to gain some perspective, I see it will be easy for him to pretend, back in London, working all hours, his bi annual visit the back of his mind. It'll be so easy to subconsciously pretend that Dad is still here.

I look towards mum, holding Dad's hand up, so his fingers encase hers. For us, I feel, it will be impossible. This is not just a bereavement of Dad; this is grief for life, as we know it. A whole new start, yet we didn't ask for it or desire it. We certainly don't need it. It's going to be tough.

In the conservatory mum shifts, I'm working on my auto pilot again, and my manners have disappeared. My etiquette at funerals not polished, I decide today is one day I am not going to worry about anyone else's feelings except the immediate family. Not because I don't want to, because I quite simply can't.

"Come sit with your Dad Tins, your Grandma and Granddad have just arrived, I better go see them."

Mum's mum and dad. Dad being an orphan since his Dad passed a couple of months ago.

I sit in the chair and take Dad's hand. Nora is wailing in the background, telling anyone who'll listen that she can't handle seeing my Dad alive, she'll remember him as he was.

I have an urge to tell her that he grew to the age of fifty, where she'd be remembering a thirty year old, yet I realise it would be unkind. Dad loved his sister, despite being nearly a stranger to her now.

I look behind my shoulder and realise all that can hear me is Dad's family, so I start muttering to Dad, as I would have, had he been alive.

"Aunty Steph's got her eye on your van Dad; hope mum wakes up and tells them to Bugger off."

He doesn't answer, so I raise his arm a touch, and take the squeeze as agreement.

"I don't know what to do with mum; will you take care of her?"

"Mickey's not sleeping properly, what do you think it is?"

"Should I open the shop on Monday?"

Without Dad's answers our conversation is a series of questions. I feel selfish hogging all the dialogue, so, in true British style I talk about the weather instead.

All the time guests, mourners, family and parasites arrive, many not showing their face since before I was born, most genuine, yet some already asking for trinkets to 'remember' Dad by.

Watches, bracelets, chains, rings. These insincere have all admired something of dad's when he's worn it, and now they're making their claim.

I hear a dealer friend, "I loved that latest leather jacket he wore, I did, he always said I could have it."

"How? He didn't know he was going to die, so how could he have said that?" I bark, swivelling my head to stare into the living room.

"I tried to buy it," the dealer admitted, "he said he might part with it one day, and I'd be the first he offered it to."

"Well he isn't parting with it today, that's for sure." Anger starts creeping in. I'm wondering how no one else can see this. How mum's still smiling, nodding, and offering this creep a cup of tea. Is it me, am I bitter?

Then another, "what happened to that watch Mike wore, about ten years ago Sylvia."

A woman this time, I've never seen her before in my life. She smiles at me as if I'm nine months old. It doesn't reach her eyes, certainly not her blue rinse.

"I've still got it, in the bureau." All eyes dart towards the dark oak-varnished Edwardian piece to my left.

Mum goes to open the top, in her own way trying to heal these peoples grief as she never can her own. I have a mental image of her throwing all Dads' jewellery up in the air, and this lot fighting to catch it, regardless of respect.

Luckily, Grandad places his hand on mums as she does. He leads her into the kitchen and away. I feel a painful stab of jealousy that mum still has her dad, but I'm grateful. His wisdom showing a diplomatic way to sort the problem, another couple of seconds and I'd have been throwing everybody out. I think Grandad realised this too.

I go back to sit with Dad, I loathe leaving him on his own, regardless of feeling lonelier than I have ever done, whilst in the presence of his corpse.

It brings no comfort. It is not my father, not anymore. Just a part of the memory that will soon be gone.

As the crisp air reminds me I'm alive, I stroke Dad's head, and notice three wiry grey hairs amongst the chocolate brown, longer than my own. They've grown, quite strangely whilst he lay in the coffin, accelerated.

I make the decision to pull them out, Dad loathed any grey hair, despite mum claiming it to be distinguished, if he were alive, he would thank me for it.

Luke and I once bought Dad an electric nose hair trimmer for Christmas, he had asked for one, he took care of himself, and hygiene was paramount. The thought now makes my ears squeeze, and my back shiver. I clench my teeth when I remember Dad exiting the bathroom, tears streaming down his face, shouting for nail scissors as the trimmer had wound and pulled his nasal hairs into a knot it wouldn't free.

Agony to watch, but as I did, as Dad swore multiple times in his London accent, I left the room and laughed. Giggled and chuckled. Once free, Dad joined me.

"That fucking thing thought I'd never get it out, nearly pulled my eyeballs out of me fucking sockets!"

I'm still laughing, seeing Dad, his face as red as a belisha beacon, eyes wide like saucers, eyebrows raised in utter shock. He now has tissue poking out of one nostril, and a tiny bit of hair out of the other.

"You've one left Dad". I point.

"Well you're just going to have to get used to it," he winces, "because I'm not shoving anything else up there till the others stopped bleeding. I'm traumatised I tell you!"

So I pull out the grey hairs with a silent smile, these memories bittersweet, and despite all psychological efforts to block them, their rain on me was torrential. From opening the front door, to putting the kettle on. Every single action during the day brought fresh memories.

I pull out two, and then reach behind Dads ear for the last, as I do, the satin lining of the coffin falls, and Dad's whole head is on full display.

I swallow some vomit as I see Dad's head covered in ugly thick black staples. No cosmetic thought has been made, as these are haphazard and roughly spaced, as if holding the scalp temporarily in place is their only purpose, and I realise sadly it is.

Dad will be cremated in less than an hour; the staples will tinkle to the bottom of the furnace, their job done.

I'm glad my Dad's not in there, but if he isn't there, where is he?

Chapter 10

I'm aware of raised whispers, the house is now full. People cannot move throughout the seventies décor without touching one another. Jacky and Ade are helping, which is comforting. Jacky gave Dad a roof over his head, when he was just twelve years old. Abandoned by his parents, thrown out by his father, Jacky and Uncle Bobby gave him the safety he needed before he was up and on his own feet and making a living for himself as a barrow boy, in Portobello Market.

His entrepreneurial skills didn't stop there. A boarded up shop on the Kings Road seemed ample opportunity for business, scouring skips for trinkets, ornaments, furniture, anything that could be cleaned up and sold again, at twelve years old, Dad was running his own second hand furniture shop.

All the time in the world, and no school to attend meant Dad could see all that London had to offer during the day. Throughout his teenage years, Dad brushed with fame so many times, he should have glittered gold, however he later told me the lifestyle wasn't for him.

He first realised the money in film making and all things movie when a director approached him as he strolled the Thames, little did Dad know, he'd stumbled across the set of the latest Doctor Who movie, and was now being paid a pretty penny to appear in it as an extra, as well as doubling up by pulling the Dalek from the water.

It seemed for a little while that the streets were paved with gold. From this chance encounter, he was asked to leave his address for payment. Having nowhere else to call his own, bar a sofa at his brothers flat, he gave the shop on Kings Road. Cynical, devoid of trust even at such an early age, he doubted they would call, yet they did.

They called, they loved the shop, they used it for another film, Up the Junction starring Dennis Waterman. Dad was discovered by the authorities and had to leg it. He was fifteen years old.

His travels took him to the other side of London, when he happened across a man loading some music equipment, speakers and drum kits, into the back of a transit van.

They were at the stage entrance to a popular London variety nightclub.

"Alright mate," Dad nodded a greeting, coming across as older than he was.

The man grunted, the equipment was heavy, he was finding it difficult to balance whilst lifting it alone.

Instinctively after Dad's years of moving furniture, Dad took hold of the amplifier, looking across to the tired man; he tried to make small talk.

"So you the roady then?"

"No, I play the drums," His accent was northern, dad couldn't place it.

"What do you do for a proper job then?" asked Dad.

"Well, this, I've been the drummer for four weeks," the man shook his head in wonderment. Dad wasn't fazed.

"You'll need a roady then?"

"Yeah, I guess we will, I'll ask the lads, but you got some muscles on you. Why not?"

Once deposited safely into the transit, with ropes tied round to hold it in place, Dad held out his hand, "Michael James".

The man took Dad's hand in his and gave it a firm shake, "pleased to meet you Michael James, I'm to be known as Ringo Starr."

The whispering got louder, mum crashing into the conservatory brings me back to the present, she takes hold of Dad's arm, people begin crowding round her.

My Gran parts the crowd like Moses with the red sea, using her electric wheelchair; she stops next to me, and whispers quite loudly in my ear.

"The hearse is here Tinsey, they need to take your dad now. Your mum needs to let go." Her voice is shaking, her tears not for the dead, but for the living, for mum, for the next difficult minutes.

"They are NOT having him!" Mum shouts. She's clinging on, as the two men from earlier walk through the garden and stand at the double doors in front of the coffin.

"He is my husband. Tina's Father. We can't live without him. He belongs HERE!"

Once again, I'm on autopilot. I would quite happily live with Dad's body for another week, yet I know we need to follow the steps; the steps are there for a reason. I'm also convinced, since the dreams, the images, the apparitions if you will that Dad isn't in there. He will show himself, with a smile, with emotion, with love. This shell held nothing of that, it barely resembled him anymore. A few days had slackened his jowls, his face even when sleeping held character, whereas dead, it held nothing but a memory.

"He's got to go at some point mum, might as well be now."

"I know!" she says, "but not yet. He's mine, not yet. I'm not ready yet!"

Her grip closes harder around Dad's arms, the pall bearers are now stood at each end of the coffin, ready to lift regardless. They must have encountered worse than this in their time. What an awful job.

The crowd start muttering, some concerned, some giggling, some discussing mum's mental health, I feel mum's the centre of a freak show, with the lack of compassion, and the vultures from earlier, I don't care if I never see anyone of them again, bar family.

"GET OUT!" I shout, "Leave my mother in PEACE. GO! GO!"

That's all it takes for the tens of people to leave, I know Aunty Sara, or Luke will be placating them, I don't care, I'm just so glad they've gone.

Gran looks at me sympathetically. She gets it.

The pallbearers begin to lift, mum's still hanging on.

"No, no , no, NO!" Mum pulls Dad's arm from the coffin, there's a snap, Grandad appears from nowhere, spins mum round, then catches her as she collapses in a heap into his chest.

I wish my Dad could do the same for me.

I sit in the back of the funeral car, staring into space, my eyes unblinking yet seeing nothing as we drive through unfamiliar territory towards the crematorium. The setting is beautiful, high on a hill, the wind fierce and bitter, and as I exit the car, I hear a few seasoned funeral goers mutter that they're relieved it's not a burial in this weather. My fingertips are numb; it's only the beginning of October.

Neil, the slimy funeral director, fusses around us, as I'd imagine Julian Clary to do.

Mum grabs my hand, it's sweaty but she doesn't seem to mind, she's come round a little bit. Luke stands at the other side.

"Here goes," we say in unison. The gardens are full of people wishing to pay their respects, yet it could be empty, we don't notice.

Sitting at the front of the chapel, we don't look behind, just cling to each other with a sick half smile on our faces, still trying to prove that we're good, we're strong, we're alright Jack. It's an act, of course it is. Dad's coffin is closed on the alter in front of us. It's not straight, as if it's just been dumped, thrown on. I guess in twenty minutes it won't matter anyhow.

I'm disappointed it's closed, as I imagined, my final farewells to be here. Knowing I'll never see him ever again, his nose, his hair, the tattoos of Indians girls on his forearms, the triangle scar on his forehead where he said he'd acquired it when he lost a game of cards, or the bite mark in his index finger, that I made when he taught me self defence at only four years old, I cried.

Chris the Priest begins his speech, he tells of Dad being a respected business man, of how he would always leave some for everyone else to make a profit, he compared him to business men of the bible. He then mentions for me to approach the pulpit and read out a short piece I have written on my memories.

I shake my head, I can't do it. I can't think about it. So Chris reads. As he does people lean forward to pat me on the shoulder. I don't know who it is, I don't care.

"Dad rarely said I love you, yet he didn't have to, as one I love you would last forever, such was our trust and faith in him. Without him, we will never feel safe or loved again."

Chris finishes and flicks the switch on the tiny CD player, the Monkeys start playing, singing "Daydream Believer."

Mum begins to hum, and it makes me smile, she hates the song. Dad's girlfriend before her, many moons ago was called Jean. So the song holds jealous memories. It shows she's thinking of me by humming to it.

I insisted on it as Dad often sang it to me, replacing Jean with Teen. I remember the most recent time, we were returning from a large antique fair in Harrogate when it came on the radio, there were boxes piled high behind our heads in the white van, dad's gear stick is temporarily fixed with a sticky fibreglass solution. We sing loudly and proudly, laughing, a strange sight to be seen by onlookers, we're having a marvellous exhausted high time, when Dad breaks quickly and a box containing several heavy pointy brass ornaments falls on my head, and knocks me off my seat and into the foot well.

Tears prick my eyes, it really hurts, yet Dad's still driving slowly, but now instead of laughing loud, he has a fit of the giggles, he's bordering on hysterical joviality. I join him, and we laugh all the way home.

"Come on Tinsey, join in." Prods mum, so I do. My voice squeaky and screechy, somehow not able to sing as well as in Dad's presence, but I make the effort.

The rollers are broken underneath Dad's coffin, so it doesn't disappear behind a curtain, it just stays there in the haphazard way it was left. People begin to leave, and pat it as they walk past. Dad would have found that quite patronising, myself, I'm reminded of having teddy bears as a young girl, and not wanting to pack them in plastic bags because I didn't think they could breathe.

I have the same feeling now about the lid on Dad's coffin, it's wrong. It seems cruel, but of course, it's just another symbol of just how very much dead he is.

As we exit, creepy Neil minces over, starts shuffling me towards the car.

"Come on now, you'll catch your death, let's have you in the car." He simpers.

I try to make myself still and solid, everyone else is still milling around, offering condolences. Some apologising for not being able to make it to the wake, I'd like to see them.

"Stop it. What are you doing? We're the last of the day, leave me, mum's not in the car yet."

He huffs, "yes but if you get into the car, everyone else will follow, I've seen them, they'll follow you, including your mother."

"But I don't want to get in the car."

"But you're shivering, look!"

I am indeed shaking, but not from the cold, from pure indignation.

Luke comes up behind, "he's right, you're shaking Tinsey, let's have you in the car."

I give up and get in. Ten minutes later we're pulling away, everybody together, when we see another hearse entering through the long sweeping driveway.

"He promised we'd be last!"

"Never mind," says mum, "done now, let's all have a drink".

"Yes, I don't think you can schedule death somehow."

Chapter 11

We arrive at the venue, a cosy but scruffy pub close to where we now live. The buffet is laid out, a few sausage rolls costing three hundred and fifty pounds according to the funeral home. The bitter pill I swallow, as this will be the first time Mother and I will be easy prey for conmen. Without Dad about it's a minefield, yet we haven't the strength to think about it now.

I've Michelle, a friend from playgroup picking Mickey up from nursery, then bringing him to me after his tea and bath. I'm grateful, yet I know I will repay this tiny favour tenfold.

Mum seems to have been swept up in a sea of sympathy, nowhere to be seen, so I approach the bar alone. Resting on the polished wood, I peruse the spirits and realise, I need to numb something. I'm not crying, I'm not terribly upset, but my thirst for alcohol is overwhelming. Instead of asking for one simple glass, I ask for the bottle instead.

"Four glasses of lemonade and the bottle of Smirnoff please."

The barmaid eyes me with suspicion, she knows it's my father who's passed and is now weighing up the responsible course of action without causing too much of a scene.

She hesitates, I start to strum my nude fingernails on the bar, I need numbing quick.

She scans the room for other members of my family to help, to make the decision for her, but all she sees is Uncle Bobby, Ade, and Kevin Marshall. Long haired, gorgeous mature antique dealer family friend Kevin.

Altogether, they tell her. "Just give her the bottle yeah? We'll pay."

The barmaid doesn't need telling twice, I take my tray of alcohol and settle at a wobbly table in a far dark corner. The first drink feels nice, yet despite not touching alcohol since the night before Dad's death, it does nothing. Doesn't calm my nerves, numb any pain, or free the clogging from my mind.

Kevin comes over to sit with me. Although he's thirty years older, he has a presence, a presence that suggests he should be famous. As if he's lost his backing singers and groupies, but can never quite find the way back.

"Gosh, I only saw your Dad last week, bought a cast iron fire off him" He sits down without asking.

I look up, I can't help but smile, Kevin looks as though his mouth is curved upwards at the corners even when he frowns.

"Been a while since I've seen you though, can I?" He picks up the bottle of vodka to pour himself a shot, I nod.

"Do you remember, the first time I met you, you were about five or six, and you dropped your dad in it over that washstand?"

I laugh, it's tickled me, just this one memory makes it seem as though Dad is sat on the chair next to me. I feel the vodka finally warming my veins, and I laugh as I cry.

"I do, gosh, I wasn't allowed out the van on deals for ages after that, but who can blame him?" I say.

"Too right, you wouldn't like it if your little one piped up when you selling a first edition. But mummy, grandad found that for nothing at a car boot."

"It's true, you don't realise just how patient and loving your parents were until you have children of your own." I begin to stare into the distance, wondering what other lessons I'll learn, what other punishments I'll forgive Dad for, yet he won't be here for me to tell.

Kevin seems to sense me slipping, he pulls me back with a chuckle.

"You were so cute. Stamping your feet, you were more cross with your father for lying than he was with you for revealing the origin of the piece."

"I gave him a hard time alright. I seriously did."

"You were just a girl who loved her Dad. I've never seen anyone turn him into such a pushover, he was a scary man to the wrong people. A fantastically loyal friend to the right ones. I was lucky to know him."

"We all were," I agree.

"Hey," Kevin's eyes light up as if a metaphoric light bulb has switched on, "do you remember the photos?"

I nod vigorously, whilst starting on my third vodka. This evening is beginning to feel like a good night out, not a wake. The rest of the guests are insignificant.

"The ones with the fairies at the bottom of the garden?"

"Yeah, gosh, I came across a few different ones, I was a bit scared, didn't trust my own judgement. So I asked your Dad to help. Your Dad made me a lot of money."

"I remember," I say.

"I showed my gratitude by giving him the last photo, the one of Frances Griffins at the Beck with the four fairies. Taken by Elsie."

"I know, I was six at the time, Dad gave it to me for my bedroom shelf, I adored it."

"Yeah, yeah he did. I couldn't believe it when he did that. The most valuable photograph in the history of Yorkshire and England, and Mike entrusted it to a six year old girl."

"I loved that photograph!"

"Oh, I know, I know you did. Do you know how much it was worth?"

"Not really, but I believed in it, despite the rumours, I really believed in it, it's not since I grew older, and looked into it a little more, that I realised I acquired it a month after Francis died."

"Yep, she lived in Scarborough."

"Really, whereabouts? I'm only a few miles out now. Mind you, not that it matters, I lost the photograph." This fact had haunted me for seventeen years.

I never mentioned it at the time, I searched high and low, as time passed by, I did wonder why mum or dad had never asked to see it. Then later, as I researched the cuttingly fairies, I deduced that the photo was a fake.

Kevin makes a faux hang dog expression.

"It wasn't a fake."

I'm speechless. I've no reason not to believe him, used to the kind of magic aura that surrounded Dad's life.

He explains further, "your dad and I thought they must be fake too, yet when an appeal was launched on TV am for the last photograph, the one you had sitting on your bedroom shelf, we realised the similarities were astounding. So we sold it back. We made a fortune. Looking back, I maybe should have waited a little while longer, we could have made more money, but we both decided the time was right. It was your dad's photo by law, I'd given it to him, yet he still split the proceeds fifty, fifty. I never forgot it. He was a true friend."

"So I had the real photograph?"

"Yes, yes you did."

I feel a little giddy as I laugh. The whole pub quietens. Each and every one looks at me. Judging me for being disrespectful to my father. All of them, some I've never seen before, others familiar but not cosy. All judging the relationship between Dad and daughter that could result in said daughter laughing her head off over his death.

They don't get it, and I hope they never will. I wouldn't wish this array of emotions on anyone. All I know now is, talking about dad is the next best thing to having him here, and it's a remedy I want to exploit, not avoid as everyone else is doing. Kevin knew exactly what I needed, he knew who would benefit most from his wisdom, and tactful grief counselling today, and it's inspiring.

Kevin lost his wife and seven year old daughter when I was a babe in arms. A brutal murder saw him returning home to a ransacked house, his wife and daughter stabbed to death on the bed.

He didn't ring the police, he didn't try to kill himself. He shut himself in the bedroom's wardrobe and stayed there.

He may still be there now, had it not been for Dad seeing his shop closed for the third day in a row.

Affected but not phased, Dad gently coaxed him from the wardrobe, and set him on the path, which would be the rest of his life without his family.

I was told of this horrifying fact once, any effort to extract gorier or more detailed specifics met against a brick wall. Gossip coming to a halt when the truth is so close to home. So devastating, as if talking more would inflict the bad luck on our own family.

Being a parent now myself, I wonder how Kevin managed to carry on. Through mum I know, the first ten years he spent on revenge, an obsessive need for justice, he became an extra arm for the police force, never letting them forget they had a killer to catch. They never did, forget, or catch the killer.

Kevin knew exactly what I needed, I'm hoping I'll be able to show the same empathy and compassion to someone else. To him, he may well be returning an out of date favour, to me he's restored my faith in human nature.

Luke walks over, no doubt as a result of my laughter.

"You've had enough now Tinsey, I think."

He's wrong. I'm not drunk. Half of me wishes I were but it seems impossible. I'm exhausted however, and quite happy to call it a day. Tomorrow we have the task of getting out of bed, of trying to pretend life goes on. Everyone back to work, leaving us to it, we have the biggest new start of our lives ahead of us.

People begin to leave as Michelle enters with Mickey. I shake hands with strangers, thanking them with a smile for their condolences, telling them it doesn't matter.

There's Dutch Patrick, "So sorry,"

"Not your fault, nothing to be sorry about."

"I know, I was with your father when I received news my sister had died. Stood in the back of a van, I was buying a sideboard from him."

"What happened?"

"Well he helped me, man of few words, but what he did say made sense. He told me I had nothing to feel guilty about, because if I had died, and she'd carried on, she would be worrying about our last bicker just as I was."

"It's true."

"We were so distracted, we didn't realise your old cat Bubbles had crept into the sideboard."

"I know, we met you at the ferry to pick her up."

He laughs. "Keep in touch, yeah?"

"I will."

Then we have Dave, he gives me a limp handshake. Gypsy origin, but trusted by my dad, I have quite a bit of respect for him.

He doesn't start with condolences.

"You've got your dad's laugh you have. I could hear you outside."

"Oh dear, sorry Dave." I look furtively to Michelle and Mickey, Mickey's not seen me yet, he's making his way over to mum.

"No, don't apologise. Look, it may not be the right time but I wanted to ask a favour."

"Go on," I'm distracted, but in as good as mood as any considering it was my father's wake.

"Your maisonette? What's happening to it now?"

"Using it as storage I guess. I've nowhere to put the furniture. Not yet."

"Would you consider renting it to me, I've nowhere to live at the minute. I'm sleeping on an ex girlfriends couch and I'm fifty years old."

"Yeah, come see me Monday Dave, I'm opening the shop Monday. Come see me, I'll see what I can do."

"Cheers Tina, you made your Dad proud, you did."

I grow half an inch with the compliment. As he ambles away, Mickey spots me and toddles over, as fast as his legs will carry him. Michelle was supposed to be dropping him at home later, not bringing him to the Wake, I didn't want him here.

"Where's Gan dad?" His first question, he already knows at any family gathering, Dad would be the head.

"Not here darling, had to go see a man about a dog in heaven."

Michelle interrupts.

"Look I'm sorry for having him back early, just my Louis, he's playing up, I've been called into school today, they think he needs anger management, I just don't know what to do with him."

Louis is Michelle's second eldest boy, at thirteen he was fast becoming a tearaway, yet I liked him, and he respected me. I was lucky; he didn't respect many adults, especially his teachers.

"What's Louis think?" I ask.

"Well, he'd rather try boxing club first. He's old enough now. I'd love him to go, but with three other kids, it's difficult to get him there."

Now, for a fact, if Dad was alive, he'd be over my shoulder, whispering in my ear that I have enough on, that I'm not to be taken advantage of; I find it difficult to say no. It's a speech impediment.

"When's he got to go?"

"Weekly, would you take him? It would mean the world to me, please. I'll look after Mickey whilst you take him."

I agree, it'll keep me busy, I need it. Why not.

"I suppose I could, not like I've an active social life, what night?"

"Monday, Wednesday and Friday."

"Three nights a week?"

"It would make his life."

"Give me a couple of weeks to sort mum out, and I'll do it."

She picks up Mickey, and plonks him in my arms as Dad's brothers come over to hug me. Uncle Billy hands me a packet of wine gums, a staple of our family diet. Loved by all of Dad's family, dad always had a paper bag full next to his comfy chair.

"Come on, let's go make vodka smoothies at home, when Mickey's in bed." says Uncle Billy.

Tall, lanky, with a kind smile but a gangster face. He's wearing a pin stripe suit which only adds to the son of the godfather impression.

Uncle Bobby and Auntie Jacky are soon by his side, I can't see Ade anywhere.

"Blimey," says Uncle Bobby, "I had to stop myself from slapping your Mickey then Teenz."

I laugh, as I know he's joking.

"Why?" I ask.

"That's all I used to do to your dad when he was that age, they're identical."

"Keep him away from Nora," chirps Billy, "she'll want to rub Vim in his hair to make it whiter, she treated him like a life size doll she did."

It becomes so clear, that Dad was the baby of this family, and as such, a freak of nature for dying. Nobody expected this, no one.

This should never have happened, he should never have died.

I can't help but set the cogs in motion for the most prominent question when grieving for a loved one.

"What If?"

Chapter 12

I'm still pondering the "What If" question a week later. I've returned to the shop, against everyone's advice, yet somehow, my soul has left it for the time being.

Dave has moved in the maisonette, on the understanding that I can use the loo and kitchen whilst I work. It's been a few days only yet already there are piles of dog do from his untrained Jack Russell whenever I enter. A mountain of crusty dinners plates, dog hair and cigarette ash covering every surface, and the furniture I've left behind chewed beyond recognition. I've cleaned when the shops been empty, which for this time of year is commonplace, yet, he never takes a hint.

I know with an absolute certainty that if Dad were alive Dave would not dare take advantage as he is, yet he's not. Dad's brothers are back down south, my own, despite promises to visit every weekend has already cancelled the next four, there's just mum and I.

Mum. Such a fragile state. Alternating between complete hyperactivity and laziness. Relying a little too heavily on alcohol to see her from day to day, making a few too many prayers to goodness knows whom, for them to take her too.

Now and again, a little flash of mum comes back, and it's comforting to know she's still there, for now, I cook, I feed and I clean hoping this will cure all else.

With a little too much time on my hands, and no one to fill the gaps, I ponder.

"What if the ambulance hadn't been twenty minutes late?"

"What if I'd listened better when Dad told me he felt tired in an afternoon?"

"What if I'd marched Dad back to the doctors when they diagnosed him with indigestion?"

"What if I'd stayed over for the antique fair, maybe I would have noticed whilst mum was heating up dinner in the kitchen?"

"What if I'd insisted on a full medical, if I'd listened more at the book fair?"

As the day wears on I'm convinced dad's number wasn't up. I'm driving myself insane with all the questions, doggedly tormenting myself with situation after situation. A part of my emotional state, my brain if you will, wants to process events logically. This new puzzle needs a solution, and whilst asking the questions, however painful, my conscious mind is telling me that if I get the correct answer, the puzzle will be solved, and everything will be ok.

Except it won't. It never can be. Dad can't come back to life no matter how much time I invest in this mystery, I haven't looked that far ahead though, so for now the questions continue, right until bedtime.

The days are drifting into a blur, I turn the light off in the bedroom. Mickey is snoring soundly on the right hand side of the double bed. The curtains are wide open, and the light from the traffic's headlights outside gives an intermittent glow. I've the window open slightly at the top, so the traffic can be heard. Lately I like to feel that people keep on living, keep on going as normal. My back is rested against the large oak headboard; I'm hunched in my duvet, my left arm free to hold a cigarette. I never used to smoke in bed; however, the bedroom seems the only place I can relax since leaving my home. The chill in the air is biting my nose, I like it. I'm staring at the curtains moving slowly in the breeze, my mind almost blank. Staring at fixed objects has become commonplace in the last two weeks. A single thought, event, or situation sending me reeling backwards into the past. My mind receiving hugs from memories long gone. A safe place.

Tonight though, it's not so safe, I've not gained any satisfaction from them and I'm no closer to solving the riddle. My frustration manifests itself in tears when I hear a voice.

"Stop It".

It's Dad.

I know no one will hear me above the traffic and the TV downstairs, so I don't feel foolish when I ask.

"Stop what? The smoking?"

I see a haze, a haze that I've not seen for years. A particularly hot summer, the waves rose from the tarmac of our road. This haze is taller, in the shape of my dad, yet I don't see him.

"No, the thinking."

"I can't stop thinking Dad, it's all I have left of you."

"No, it isn't. Close your eyes. I want to show you something."

"Where?"

"The garden, we always meet in the garden. Close your eyes, picture it. You'll see it."

So I do. It's smaller than I first imagined. I begin my journey to it by walking down worn polished wide limestone steps. There are stone banisters on either side, trees pruned to follow the flow as I descend.

When I reach the bottom I am stood on a lush green lawn, there is topiary everywhere. Hedges in cones, candy twists, triangles, squares, balls, no animals though. I can hear water and assume it's from a babbling brook just out of sight. My dad is stood waiting.

His hair is all grey. I find this odd. He also has a new haircut. Odder still.

"Tell me who cut your hair dad and I'll get them for you",

Dad smiles as if I'm being too silly, he'd have laughed heartily at even the slightest joke when he was alive. It seems he has something serious on his mind.

"We're not here for that Tinsey. It's the questions; you need to stop punishing yourself. I can help."

"What questions?"

"The what if? Of course if I'd gone back to the doctors, I may have been saved, but I didn't. Just like any person who is knocked down by a bus, or in the wrong place at the wrong time, ending in their death. Regardless of circumstance, our number was up."

"So everyone in 9/11 their number was up?"

"I can't answer that, but I'd say so, yeah. They're good people. It's not those you should be sad for, it's the ones they left behind."

"I can understand that."

"I knew I was going to die Tinsy, I did. I was 90% certain. Ten percent of me thought I was being a hypochondriac, but I knew my time had come. I was never meant to grow old."

"No, I can't imagine you old."

"I'd have hated living but being dependant on others too, you know that."

"I do. But mum. Poor mum."

"I know. You'll help her, I can't get through I don't know why. Maybe it would be too much. Tell her, about the garden."

"I will."

"So right now, I want to show you something, I want us to do something. It may seem strange but it will answer a lot of your questions, and hopefully remove the bitterness."

"I trust you Dad, I always have."

"Always?"

I know Dad's referring to the one and only adult argument we had where I disbelieved a point he made, it was not long before he died. I regret it every day.

"I was in a bad mood; I shouldn't have taken it out on you."

"I know me neither."

I'm walking alongside Dad, until we reach a structure resembling a mausoleum, except there's nothing morbid about it, only beautiful.

It only has half a roof, the clematis and honeysuckle creeping up the walls makes it seem as if this is how it is meant to be.

We enter, there's one solitary stone pew, the rest is empty. Spotlessly clean.

"Sit down," dad motions with his hand, I take a seat, it's comfortable, Dad sits to my left.

"Right this may seem odd, but we can bend time and space here. Objects are what we want them to be, do you understand?" He asks slowly, as if talking too fast would make my brain explode with the information.

"Kind of, but if everything's the way you want it to be, why the hell did you choose that hair?"

Dad smiles as if I've not quite got it.

"I didn't, you did. Believe me, when I look in a mirror, I'm twenty five years old again, some part of you, wanted to see me old, and older than I was when I died."

I realise I have been thinking a lot about how Dad would look if he were left to age. The answer satisfies me for the time being, so I shrug.

"So now," says Dad, "we're going back to the time when I died. Yet this time you'll be present. Not your mum. Just me and you. I'm going to take it to the two hours before, so you can be prepared. You know what's going to happen. Twenty past four, ok?"

"What if I manage to save you?"

"We'll discuss that if it happens, now can you see the clock?" Dad points to a high point above the entrance, a basic white plastic kitchen clock with large black numbers appears.

"I see the clock, its ticking."

"Nothing else it knows how to do but tick along, time. Now, what else do you need?"

"A telephone." I'm getting into the swing of this now. My heart's beating a little faster, as if I'm on a live version of the Krypton factor, the thought of actually winning, overwhelming.

The telephone appears. This is also white, plastic, and basic. I'd have thought I would have imagined a black Bakelite 1950's phone, but no.

I move over to the phone, and immediately dial 999. Dad is sitting comically, watching the clock, his back straight, hands folded in his lap.

It rings once and then someone answers.

I quickly give mums address, and then they ask what the problem is.

"My father, he has chest pains, I need someone here."

"Can he breathe?" the voice crackles on the other end.

"Yes."

"Can he walk and talk?"

"Yes."

"Can you put him on the phone?"

"I could."

"I think you should drive to A&E. there's a wait but this doesn't seem too urgent."

"But he will die of a heart attack in ninety minutes?"

"You can't possibly know that, take him to your nearest hospital. I'll phone ahead tell them you're coming."

The line goes dead.

"Aspirin," I mutter. Aspirin appears. Yes, you guessed it, plain white bottle. Clean and shiny though. Minimalist look here.

I give Dad four to be on the safe side. As well as his heart attack, Dad developed a blood clot. This should thin his blood. I've read about it.

"I'll ring them back in half an hour, ask them to come." I say to no one in particular.

Then a thought dawns on me? "Am I allowed to take you to Scarborough Hospital?"

"Of course," answers Dad, "just imagine it."

I'd driven Dad to the hospital against his wishes only two months before. Whilst moving house, he tore the ligaments in his left arm as he lifted a juke box from his van. His arm was a bloody mess, only on the inside. It was plain to see.

I remember telling Dad that he needed to have it checked out, or he could die.

"Don't be so silly," he'd said.

"I'm serious Dad, a blood clot could form. Blood clots are serious. "

I scared him enough for him to hop in the car and let me take him to the minor injuries unit.

I need not have bothered. The Asian doctor told him to go away and rest it.

We both left feeling a little foolish. It contributed to his death.

So here we are again, the hospital, the waiting room. There are others walking around, when we are called through to a cubicle.

Dad is told to remove his shirt, and lay on a stretcher, with a pulse monitor on his index finger. He obliges without a word. The nurse disappears and leaves us alone. The same white clock is on the wall just outside the drawn curtain, we've twenty minutes left.

Neither of us wants to start an in depth conversation as Dad's due to die any minute, we don't want to be mid sentence. So we stick to the light stuff.

"She'll have gone to get those sticky things Dad."

"Yep."

The nurse does come back; she places a band around his arm that begins to inflate, as it does, she rustles behind the curtain before wheeling in a new machine.

When the band deflates, the first machine beeps and flashes. Without a single change of her facial expression, the nurse continues with her job.

"These might feel a little cold, but if you can just relax and breathe normally, we can monitor your heart rate."

Once Dad's all stickered up, she leaves for barely a second before she returns with a doctor.

"Well, Mr James," he begins, "seems you've had some activity in the heart region of late. Have you noticed any shortness of breath, chest pains, and numbness in one or both arms?"

"Yes," Dad nods. "Only last week, I was saying to Tinsey, I was stuck at a car boot, I had all of that, I had to get out, I couldn't breathe. I thought it was claustrophobia and a panic attack."

"Most definitely a heart attack." Says the doctor.

I wait for my Dad's answer, but there is none, when I look over he's gasping for breath.

"Oxygen quick!" orders the doctor. "Take him to resus, NOW!"

I'm pushed out of the way by the stretcher, at least three more nurses, and one doctor arrive to follow dad's stretcher. It's made clear I am not allowed to follow.

A strange feeling for someone watching their loved one die, but at this minute, I feel quite serene. I have complete trust in the doctors, and know he could not be in better hands. He has to survive.

If only, if only the ambulance crew had arrived earlier. Mum tortured herself with this daily now.

It's a full half an hour before anyone talks to me again. It's the doctor. The first one.

"Would you like me to call anybody?"

His first words.

"Why?" I ask.

"I'm very sorry, but we couldn't save your father. We helped him past the heart attack, but we couldn't find what else was stopping him breathe."

"It was a blood clot, " I say.

"The post-mortem will tell us," he carries on regardless, "but if it were a blood clot, once this size, even if we'd been perfuming open heart surgery at the time, we still wouldn't have been able to save him."

As he finishes the sentence, the whole hospital drifts away. Dad and I are once more in the garden. This time sitting on the grass. Dad lies on one elbow, and chews a piece between his teeth. His hair is a dark brown again.

"Do you see?" he asks between chews. He seems much calmer and happier now.

"Yes, I do. Mum though, when will mum see."

"In time, you need to tell her."

"I'll try, it's not easy."

"No. Your mum will have to let go sometime, although she is destined to be with me. You though, you need to live your life. Get out there, stop being so scared."

"I know," and before I can ask what Dad meant about mum, he's gone, and so am I.

Chapter 13

I have a blissful moment when I awake the next morning, where I think Dad is still alive, and then, like every other morning, the thunderbolt hits, and winds me before I've even had my first cup of coffee.

No matter how many times I speak to him, dream about him, nothing replaces him being here. One death and everything has changed. My whole life, even my business. The balance has been knocked out, and there seems no way of getting back on track.

Tonight I've agreed to take Louis to boxing. The evening beckons. After the nursery run and snacks, I have an overwhelming urge to collapse in a hot bath with a good book. Mondays are hard enough without sustaining the forced motivation past five pm, however, Mickey having watched Rocky with me last week, is already running up and down the staircase with a towel around his neck, Louis is due to arrive any second. I tell myself I'm spending an hour at the gym, nothing more, and my mind is set.

It takes a little while to find the oversized port-cabin. Hidden deep in the estate which is infamous for its mafia like population, we venture through the houses in the dark and cold, already feeling as if our resolve is being tested. Mickey's bravado has gone, without the cocoon of our home, he now clings to my forearm, as if he were a drowning boy.

We reach our final destination and are greeted by trainer Tommy, 56, who is so similar to the trainers in the movies, I look around for a young Sylvester Stallone.

Michelle pipes up, "my friend would like to join in too, for fitness."

Tommy looks me up and down, a cruel sneer on his face. I don't know about boxing, but I'd like to participate in a little slapping right now.

"No way, no, no women, never, I don't agree with it. It's a bloody FREAK show, women out there, trying to box like men. Nope, nada, NO!"

I'm scared he's going to do himself damage, with a wave of my hands I assure him, I'm really not that passionate about it. I only wanted to do a bit of skipping, that's all. He storms away, I've insulted his core beliefs. Ashamed of myself I skulk to the sidelines, and gently nudge Louis towards the circle of men warming up far side of the ring.

As Michelle flirts with the boxers, my maternal instincts surface when I see Louis having an attack of the nerves. Tears springing at the corner of his eyes. It's a scary environment. Most are men, twice his size. The gym itself smells of plaster dust and sweat. The floorboards are bare, and the stuffing is poking out of the seventies style chairs. An artist has painted patches of sound wall with images from well known fights. Holes have been covered with second hand mirrors, and newspaper articles. It's not a place to relax in. So I join the circle next to him to help him relax. I'm showing him what to do, when a bell rings and the trainers bark simultaneously, "RUN!". Louis, suitably relaxed sets off with the others; I walk back towards the seats.

"No, no, no, girly" growls Tommy, "up you get, you want to train, you are going to train!"

For a few seconds I wrestle with myself. I don't have to take that attitude from anyone. I'm a grown independent woman. I left the bullies behind at primary school, and have no desire to revisit the personality war endured with my games teacher. I am self-employed for good reason.

I start to laugh it off, to walk away, to join Michelle and Mickey in the safeness of the uncomfortable seats, when another desire takes control, a need I never imagined, a need for this man's respect. Somehow, it seemed a more mature way of wiping the smirk off his face than a slap ever would, so I run.

The first lap is easy, I'm smiling, enjoying it, piece of pie, bring it on.

"Drop, give me twenty!" Shouts Lenny. I've yet to make his acquaintance, but he seems happy enough. Eighty two years old and former trainer of Paul Ingle. The North Yorkshire Boxer that went professional. Quite the mini celebrity, so Michelle informs me.

After the press ups, we're running again. Punching the air, punching forwards, sidestepping, hopping, trying to keep my knees up, ten minutes later I feel as if I'm going to vomit. My mouth is dry, my breath, so heavy it takes what little moisture is left on my tongue as I exhale. Each inhalation brings plaster dust. My chest is thumping, my body white hot. I welcome the rivers of perspiration that are running down my back, from my forehead, into my eyes. Momentarily blinding me as it mixes with the mornings mascara. We must be stopping soon. This is torture.

Just as I feel I'm going to have to walk out or collapse, he tells us to walk. I look over to Michelle who is holding a bottle of water, draining it with my eyes. Mickey is sat next to her, no rosy cheeks, nothing, seems he gave up quite a few laps ago. Louis looks in the same state as me.

After five minutes walking I feel confident enough to talk, I walk over to Michelle and Mickey, she hands me the water as she shakes her head in a , "you're mad," gesture.

As I put the bottle of water to my lips, Tommy walks up behind,

"No time for that," he murmurs in my left ear, then to the entire gym he shouts, "Skipping ropes, NOW!"

I grab Louis as my security blanket, and we both take the scraggy ropes that are left hanging limply from a nail in the wall. The others are already skipping. Some so fast it is a blur. I feel confident I can do this. Girls skip better than boys. Back straight, head held high, I turn to Louis beside me.

"Just copy Auntie Tina, darling, you'll soon get the hang of it, you'll see."

He waits as I swing the rope speedily over my head, I jump, too early, and stumble onto a flying rope in front. It stings the tip of my nose as my knees connect with the floor.

Lenny walks over, he's laughing so hard the boys don't know whether to skip or watch. I think I've just achieved my personal best of how many times in an hour I want the ground to swallow me up.

He doesn't introduce himself, just stands behind me, grabs my hands.

"Your arms, they shouldn't move. Spin from the wrist. Jump from the balls of your feet, your heels should never touch the ground unless I say so. Now, try."

I try it, and manage two skips in succession. My ten stone frame makes it feel like I'm lifting a baby elephant every time I jump.

He walks away swinging his head. Still chuckling.

The skipping ends, absolutely shattered, I see everyone choosing boxing gloves. I think the girls part is over, so again try to flee to Mickey, half way there I'm dragged back.

"You're pretty fit girly", sneers Tommy. "Get some gloves on; let's see what we can do with you."

I notice everyone has wraps on their hands; however, I'm not here for the boxing, only the training, and the fitness. It seems, however, that I am going to learn whether I like it or not. I can't walk away now.

I don some gloves. They scratch my knuckles, they itch, they smell of sweaty feet, and I have an urge to keep banging them together. They do feel right.

Tommy holds a punch bag steady.

"Ok, so you're right handed. I want you to hit the bag with your left."

I stand square onto the bag. I punch with my left. My feet do not move. Even I know it's pretty pathetic.

I feel hands on my shoulders behind me. It is Lenny.

"Here, left foot forward." He shifts my weight, so I'm sideways on.

Right foot parallel to Tommy, left foot pointing forwards. My face is looking straight at the bag, but my body is facing the other side of the gym.

"That's it, "he encourages," now, hands up, protect your face. Let's have a look at your right hook, ignore him."

Tommy shakes his head, but he's not walked away, he's still holding the bag.

I go to hit the bag, but have to move my whole body forwards to do so.

Tommy groans. I don't know what I've done wrong.

"Here," says Lenny, placing me back into position. "The whole point of this is so you don't have to move or lose balance. Twist at your waist. Bring your shoulder forward. Use the force of your shoulder to hit. Not your hand. Try again."

I try to quickly store all the information he's given me, I feel too tired to think, however, I seem to have the technique in sequence, as I pull back my shoulder a little before striking. I can feel the force, and I'm impressed with the power. It moves the bag and Tommy with it. He clips me around the ear as it does.

"Keep your defences up! No good a punch like that if you leave your face wide open!"

"Brilliant," whispers Lenny.

An hour later, I feel I've mastered about one percent of what is an extremely complicated yet invigorating sport.

I'm about to leave, children in tow, and yes, towel round my neck, as Lenny beckons me over.

He's holding his hand out. Tommy is watching from the ropes of the ring.

"A key," he offers, "to your own changing room."

He leads the way to the store cupboard. I'm honoured. I didn't expect to be rewarded for being an overprotective Aunt.

"Go home," he orders, "think about it. If you want to become a boxer, I will train you. You must be dedicated, and willing to work hard."

I daren't tell him tonight was for fitness only, it's a fact both trainers seemed to have missed. They really do believe I've gone to train to be a boxer. Real bona fide amateur boxer. I consider putting Lenny right, but believe I would be lying if I did.

In just two hours I feel as though I've grown six inches. I've gained an identity, separate from single mother, businesswoman, I've secured my own slice of life. There's passion coursing through my veins, fortunately not for some unsuitable suitor.

In one swift selfish moment, I had already made up my mind to a question I never thought I would be asked less than two hours ago,

"I don't need to think Lenny, I want it. More than Brad Pitt waiting for me at home, I want it."

"Good girl," he says patting me on my wet back, " see you on Wednesday, the fun starts here!"

As I return home, I'm giddy, I have a purpose, I have a slice of life again.

I'm eager to tell mum about my new passion, my new lease of life.

Bouncing up and down on the spot, the adrenalin coursing through my veins, I jibber, as Mickey playfully punches my knees.

"I can't wait until Wednesday mum; it's fantastic, absolutely brilliant. Wow, and I could box, I could really truly box." I'm grinning whilst shadow boxing in front of the live fire.

"Don't talk stupid Tina, whatever would your father think? Do you seriously believe I want to lose another family member? Deliberately putting yourself in harm's way like that, you're crazy."

Maybe she's right, I deflate. I'm back, to good old solid grief.

Chapter 14

When I enter the shop the next morning, the usual smells assault me. Before Dave moved in, I adored opening the door to the smell of coffee, (albeit set up by myself), books, leather and words. An invigorating way to start any morning, but today I smell cheap stale whisky, dog dirt, wet dog, and nicotine.

I leave the shop door open as I step in, the bells tinkling in the wind, the shop needs some air.

I'm aching madly from last night's activity, I'm tired physically and mentally, yet I'd rather be here than anywhere else, I can lose myself here. This is my territory. The door chimes shake a little louder and a woman, who's known by me to be a little difficult, breezes in behind me before I've even reached the till and the light switches. Bookshops can be quite dark no matter how bright the day.

I'm not officially open for another half an hour yet this doesn't seem to bother her.

"I want to complain. I want compensation. I want my money back." She demands.

I flick on the lights, and look her in the eye and sigh. This is not the first time.

"Calm down, I'm sure we can sort out whatever the problem. They're books after all, what can you have possibly found wrong with the books?" Unhappy ending? I think, unkindly to myself.

She reaches into her handbag and pulls out a paperback with an empty floppy spine.

"I didn't realise until I got home, and began reading it, that there's pages missing."

Rubbish, no one would even pick up a book to read that looked like that, a blind person would tell it was off just holding it. I certainly would not shelve a book that looked like that, let alone sell one. If this awkward woman had shopped here since Dad's death, I may be questioning myself, my own little world has become a little too comfortable to leave of late, but she hasn't, so she's pulling a fast one. I'm a more than a little annoyed at her cheek and feel well within my rights when I reply,

"I'm sorry, but this shop would not sell such a book, certainly not in this ragged state. I think something must have happened at home. Surely you realised it was only half a book before you picked it up to read?"

"Of course I didn't," she answers hurriedly," that is exactly why I think I deserve compensation for the three hours I wasted reading the first seven chapters before it came to an abrupt halt."

I'm almost speechless, yet not quite. I wouldn't dream of demanding this from anyone, I'd sure like a little of this ladies confidence.

"I will refund you for the book, and give you another copy, free of charge so you can finish what you started, how about that?"

"Not good enough, I want my compensation."

I try to keep my temper in check. I do not believe a word of this woman, always a little difficult, and quite the bully. I find her intimidating, yet usually with dad around that's all it was. Today I almost feel a bit scared. I raise myself up to my entire five foot two, and begin an attempt of standing up for myself.

"I am sorry madam that was a generous offer. I would never have sold a book in that condition, let alone allow it to cross my threshold, I think you are fabricating the truth a little, and if you won't take a book as compensation, there's really nothing else I can offer you."

I take a lung full of air, and breathe out. I'm shaking a little, as I always do when I'm slightly angry, or at the sign of injustice. I despise confrontation and make every effort to avoid it, always.

I think I've finally gotten through, I'm proud of myself, yet the woman in her silence, the middle-aged bespectacled wild haired woman is staring at a patch of floor to my left between two high bookshelves. The children's section.

I follow her gaze and find devastation of the worst kind, books chewed, pages ripped, hundreds beyond repair, and the cherry on the top is a huge Jack Russell turd.

I want to cry. I'm defeated.

"How much?" I ask the woman.

"Ten pounds should do it, and I won't mention this to anyone."

I open the till and hand her twenty. "Take this, and never shop here again."

Pleased as punch, she leaves. I follow her to the door and resist the urge to trip her up, no doubt she'll be singing all the way home. I close the shop door, and get to work cleaning up the mess.

I've stuffed the ruined books into the blue recycling bin, shedding a tear for each one. As used books, each one held a special place for me, an auction I bid at, a customer I bought them from. If a customer requested a book one week, I would add it to a list and scour the internet, charity shops or car boots for it, as a lot of books are now out of print, I have customers all over the UK that adore this extra service. This pile of books would take months to replace, and that all depends on how lucky I am. I may never find some again. I'm contemplating sitting on the lid so it closes, when my wind chime indicates someone has opened the front door. I was in such a rush this morning, I've not yet had a cup of coffee, my mind is not functioning, I ache from last night's gruelling work out, and my knuckles look as if I've been scraping them along the floor as I walk, which right now, I could happily do.

I'm slightly relieved when I discover it's a professional man with a briefcase. Hopefully too busy to hang around, quick choice and away.

I dust off my hands, as I protect myself behind the counter, my psychological barrier.

"Hello there Miss James," the man holds out his hand for me to shake, "I'm Ian from Tran global advertising, and I couldn't help but notice that you needed a little more of that yourself."

He spins around in the empty shop. I already know I haven't the spare cash for advertising right now, we're ticking along ok thank you very much.

"I'm sorry, it's the wrong time for me," I try on my most assertive but friendly voice, "I don't need advertising right now."

Ian smiles at me as if I'm a little backwards.

"But Miss James, even Richard Branson needs advertising right now. Every business needs advertising for it to stay afloat, to make money, to ignore this is quite simply stupidity, and if I may say so, a detriment to the future of your charming little shop."

He's right, I haven't the energy for this mental sparring.

"I just can't afford it right now." I try a different approach.

"Well that's where I come in, this is completely affordable, better still, I can arrange it so we take only one payment now, and another at Christmas, when business is a little, um, faster, yes?"

This man has an answer for everything.

"Look leave your details, I'm very busy, I'll have a read and contact you if I'm interested." My customers obviously don't read, as this is the second person who has entered, with a closed sign on the door, directly above the opening times of the shop. It's a true testament to the nature of the person; Ian confirms this by continuing,

"No can do, sorry. I've only got these advertising spaces today, they'll be gone after today. Today they are half price. You'd be a fool to miss out."

"I'll have to miss out then, sorry."

He's not put off, and he hasn't closed his briefcase either,

"Tell me the reason why, and I'll help you see how much it will benefit you."

I give up. Half an hour later, Ian is grinning like a Cheshire cat, a new cheque for two hundred pounds in his pocket, and a direct debit instruction for quarterly payments. I'd ring Dad right now, tell him what a fool I've been, ask him to sort out my mess, cry on his shoulder, it still seems alien not to have this, as if I've not quite processed it yet. Realising it would leave a huge hole, with me teetering on the edge, scared to fall in.

For the next couple of hours, I take advantage of the bad weather and the subsequent lack of customers. The rain is torrential outside, so armed with bin bags, and disinfectant, I set to work on the house. I know this is not my job, yet I cannot make a cup of tea with a kettle stuffed with hairs and lime scale, or relieve myself on a toilet bowl whose interior colour doesn't match the exterior. Yuck.

I made the decision to move out the night Dad died, at the funeral I found out Dave was looking for somewhere immediately, so we have come to an agreement. Dave generously lets me use Mickey's old bedroom for storage, which is a godsend.

I make my way to the top of the house, with a view to picking up our bedding and electrical blankets. I have my bin bags, and feel quite relaxed knowing I will be taking more little luxuries back to mum's house. Mickey and I had missed our own bedding, our fleecy warm under blankets, it's a comfort to know, that as the rain continues tonight, we will be safe in our familiar snugness.

My old bedroom is next door to Mickey's on the top floor. Dave uses this as his own. I try not to look even though the door is wide open. It's none of my business. I see a spilt coffee cup and contents in one corner and curse under my breath, the carpet was new three weeks before Dad died. It was the carpet, which prompted my parents to make carpet enquiries of their own.

It seems the worst is yet to come though, as I'm greeted with complete devastation of an entire nursery.

The first sight I see is feathers, feathers everywhere, goose down and duck, I know this, because these are the contents of our pillows and duvet. Our very expensive pillows and duvet. Our pillows and duvet that took almost a week's wage, and will never afford again in this lifetime, ok tad dramatic, but still.

The next demonstration is chewed plastic. More particularly, wires. I follow a few and find urine soaked electric blankets. Then, a converted tiffany lamp. A farmyard animals mobile. Teddy bears, wallpaper, masticated and defecated on. Nothing in the entire room is salvageable, not even Mickey's cot.

A few weeks ago, this would have been tragic, yet now I've seen the bigger picture, it hardly matters at all. I am alive, Mickey is alive, Mum is healthy, that's all that concerns me right now. Nothing could deal a bigger blow as Dad's death. This is insignificant. Tiny. Possessions.

I put the entire contents in to six separate bin bags, and make a mental note to call my man with a van to pick it all up. Another milestone, another level of maturity.

I return to the shop with the echo of the bell. It's still pouring down outside, and as I descend the steps I wonder who would be mad enough to shop in this weather.

It's an old lady, in a see through anorak, with two small children. She brings in a wet pram, and then shakes out an umbrella so the water sprays all over my window display. You don't have to own a bookshop to know, water and books don't mix.

She walks over to hand me a book, and then takes out three packed lunches from the trolley of the pram. Finding a space in the children's area, which, now clean, looks almost normal again, they all sit in a circle and begin chewing on cheese sandwiches.

"I'm sorry, I don't allow food in the shop. Or water." I meant to say drink, water slipped out. Freudian slip.

"Read the book dear, you need to be more charitable".

I look at the faux green leather cover, and read Watchtower, The Family.

"I've seen your little boy", she continues, "your family would be quite welcome to join, we can help you overcome the death of your father."

I see the rain; my conscience will not allow me to turn these people out, despite my rules. She has the friendliest face I've seen all day, and just lately, I would relish the opportunity to be able to talk about Dad. It seems, we're not allowed to talk about him, especially with mum. Far too upsetting. I open the book, and see a picture of a conventional family. Mum, dad, son, daughter. It makes me smile a little.

The heading reads, "The only way to be a family."

I'm puzzled, so I ask the woman for clarification. She's now poking straws into cartons of drink for the children. The children are reading books from the shelves with their buttery fingers as they eat.

"Um," I tread carefully, " I'm actually a single parent, does it matter?"

She swallows her mouthful whole, "widowed?"

"No,"

"Divorced?"

"No."

"Single as in?"

"Single as in, I dumped Mickey's father because his smelly feet became unbearable during pregnancy."

"And the father is?"

"A lead guitarist in Greece last time I checked."

"Christian?"

"Not quite sure."

Without another word, the woman leaves the remains of the food scattered over the floor, bundles one child into the pram, and takes the others hand. She opens the umbrella before exiting the shop, Dave pushes past her, and the umbrella, knocking her backwards a fraction.

"I will not be bringing my children to such a house of sin ever again."

With a swish of see through anorak, she's gone.

I try to catch Dave before he disappears out again. His gigantic frame is bustling around the kitchen looking for something.

"Have you seen my knife?" He demands. This throws me off balance; I'm supposed to have the upper hand here.

"No, look, I need to talk to you, your dog."

"My father bought me that knife. You of all people should understand how important it is."

"I do, but I've not seen it, it'll turn up."

"You must have, I left it, right here, you've been bloody cleaning again. Has Mickey had it?"

"I haven't seen a knife. I certainly wouldn't let Mickey play with one."

"Oh for fucks sake woman." he shouts, opens the back door, and slams it as he grumbles up the back drive.

Our little tête-à-tête didn't go as I expected, not at all. I've had enough.

Admitting defeat for the day and needing a hug, I close the shop early and pick Mickey up. Yet far from the happy smiling face I imagined, he's whinging, and miserable. He's sensed my mood, and is displaying a tantrum I wish I could. The entire journey home is spent with Mickey screaming. Screaming so loud, until he finally wears himself out and nods off to sleep.

I silently pull the car into the drive; Dad's white van is being driven out, by no other than Aunty Steph's husband, Ronnie. Mums stood, crying, arms folded against the last drops of rain.

"What's going on mum, that's Dad's van".

"What use is it to us Tina? I can't drive it, you can't drive it. May as well let someone get some use out of it."

"It's brand spanking new, Dad only had it a few months, send it back to where he got it from. I could learn to drive it. Mobile bookshop, let's just have a bit more time, yeah."

"It's done now." Mum turns and walks back into the house as I watch his pride and joy being driven away by someone who never knew just how wonderful he was.

Chapter 15

My dreams are interrupted with a fast force, as if somebody has sat on the television remote control, changing the channel and raising the volume all at the same time. I shake in my subconscious, however, I've not long to adapt, as real or imaginary, a huge rabid dog, is galloping towards me.

It's teeth are bared, his gums covered in a milky white froth. He looks like a large sheepdog, yet I haven't the time to examine him as he flies through the air, spring boarded by his back legs, straight at my un-expecting face.

His claws catch my ear first, and as I raise my arm to defend myself, the animal's teeth sink into it. The blood pours. Everywhere. It splashes onto the tiled floor on which I'm standing. In this dream, I'm in the kitchen, getting the dog out of the house is paramount. I open the back door to the garden with my free arm, as the dog's jaws are locked on my other, growling, twisting, ripping. I'm almost expecting who I see as the fresh night air hits me.

I'm shaking the dog off, trying to free my arm, when Dad steps forward. Behind him is Grandad, smelling the flowers, walking slowly in a daze.

Dad grabs the dog by the scruff of its neck with one hand, and then opens its jaw, by putting pressure on a certain spot with his other.

I clutch my bloody arm to me; the dog is trying to spin, trying to give itself a free rein to launch its teeth at Dad. Dad's overpowering it for now.

"Thanks Dad, thank you so much." Once again, I take for granted Dad's protection of me.

"I can't keep doing this Tina; you've got to get yourself a thicker skin. For Mickey's sake, come on. For yourself." He's quite angry. I didn't expect that. I thought he would be overjoyed at seeing me again, but he's actually giving me a bollocking.

"Ok, I will, I promise," I see the dog breaking free, as it tries to swallow Dad's hand, he kicks it, none to gently, flooring the rabid creature. I scream. "Don't hurt it Dad!"

"For fucks sake Tina, just how many times do you have to be hurt before you'll fight back?"

With this, Dad slams the back door in my face, and drags the dog out of sight. My Granddad obediently follows. I wonder briefly why Granddad is there at all, as he is still alive.

The phone ringing, and mum's surprised voice wake me up. My head is pounding again, the headaches worse, I put it down to dehydration from the thrice weekly boxing sessions.

"Tinsey, it's Grandad," she shouts up the stairs, this time waking Mickey. I leave him rubbing his eyes, as I take my heavy head to mums spot, the chair.

She has her ear to the phone, and is uming and ahing, as if she never shouted me down at all. Assuming the moment has passed, I take myself into the kitchen, to start making my first cup of coffee.

"Tina, will you come here, it's your Grandad!" Mum sounds a little impatient.

I curse under my breath before every detail of my dream comes flooding back to me. My heart starts thudding, not so much for myself, but my mum. Losing her father, I wouldn't wish it on anyone, no matter how old. On top of Dad, mum wouldn't cope. It would see her off, most definitely. With trepidation, I stand in front of her as if expecting the sting from a headmaster's cane.

"What's the matter?" I ask.

"He wants to talk to you, here." and she offers me telephone. I gingerly take it, and put it to my ear, as mum walks away, muttering something about Granddad finally cracking up under her breath.

I hear the clatter of spoons and porcelain, and hope mum is finishing off my coffee, as my mouth is so dry I can hardly speak. I'm also feeling extremely sorry for myself after last night's dream. Dad should know I need comforting, not scolding. I'm furious and confused, all rolled into one.

As the sounds continue in the kitchen, I take mums vacated seat. The grieving chair as I call it mentally. It's still warm, I tuck my feet beneath me and notice how much safer I feel, curled into a ball in it. It still smells of dad. Dad and a little of mum's Chanel no.5.

"You THERE?" Echoes the handset. It's Grandad, not only is he partially deaf, he thinks everyone else is too.

"I'm here Granddad, turn your volume up!"

"My WHAT?"

"Your volume on your phone." I'm pointing to the same button on my phone, but he can't see it, so I don't know why I think this might help.

He seems to have sussed it anyway.

"Who am I talking to?" He shouts still.

"Tina."

"WHAT? Samantha?"

"Tina!"

"Sylvia?"

"TINA!"

"Oh Tina, right I wanted a word with you."

My body slouches, relaxing now we've confirmed identities. I'm so glad he's still alive.

"Go on Grandad." I'm not sure if he hears me or not, but I talk anyway.

"Last night, don't tell anyone, but I think I had an outer body experience."

He pauses, waiting for my gasp, but I'm not forthcoming. Little shocks me anymore; I'm becoming quite passive to it all. He continues,

"I met up with your Dad." My gasp comes. What if? Was he?

"Where Grandad, where?"

"In your mum's garden, well no, it was another garden first, then your mums, don't know what happened there. Tell her the cyclamen are looking good though."

"Ok." I'm almost speechless.

"Actually don't. No. No. just you, can only talk to you."

"Ok."

"Anyway, I saw you there, with that bloody dog."

"Yeah, it bit me." The gushing of blood not so dramatic now I'm awake and unharmed.

Mum puts a coffee on the table beside me; she raises her eyebrows, silently asking what the hell I'm talking about. I swirl my fingers near my ears, and smile as if Grandads having a loopy episode, she seems satisfied, and walks into the conservatory for a smoke. The sound of the trains and traffic in there, she wouldn't be able to hear.

"That was your dad showing you."

"Showing me what? How to catch rabies?"

"No, he's annoyed, at himself, not at you. He's annoyed that he wrapped you up in cotton wool, that he protected you so much, that now you have to go it alone, you're hurting."

"So he's annoyed that he loved me?"

"No, that's not what I said, and you know it. Now stop being so petulant."

Second bollocking in two days, marvellous. I'm trying to cope with a major tragedy here. I feel as if I want to tell my Granddad to get lost and leave me alone, as I would have done had I been four years old. It's a strong urge, and it's only when he speaks again, that I hang on.

"He loves you so much, he thought you were ready, he thought you were strong. You have always been a survivor, and he thought put to the test, you would fight. It seems you're not though."

"I'm using all my strength fighting every day. Waking up on a morning. I've nothing left."

"Yes you have. This is what you don't realise. Yes, you have. You are an amazing woman, if only, if only you would stand up for yourself, and stop being so damn scared. We need you, all of us."

"Why can't Luke be the strong one?"

Grandad titters a little but not unkindly.

"Luke has his own life now. His own family. It has to be you."

"So what do I do?"

"Fight back, just fight. Soon you won't have to, but until then, keep fighting, for you, for Mickey, just fight."

"I'm scared."

"That's why it's so hard, but soon, you won't be scared anymore."

"What about you? What were you doing in the garden? Why were you with Dad? Are you dying?"

"We're all dying Tina. At which rate, depends on fate."

"Ok, clever sod, are you dying this year?"

"No, no I think I'll be here for Christmas, I've already bought you all toffees. I was just wandering really, having a look. I didn't know I could do it. Apparently I can."

"Will you do it again?"

"No, not if I want to give you all your toffees, and sample your Christmas dinner. Thought I'd come to you this year."

I smirk, as when Grandad had spent Christmas with us when dad was alive, there was always a battle over the remote control, and Dad's chair.

"So if you do it again, you'll die?" I'm so curious, it seems Grandad happened upon Dad by accident, I want to be able to see him when I choose, not only when Dad chooses. I'm so keen to clear the air, I'd quite happily practice a bit of floating right now.

"I don't know, I could. See when I left my body, well it was odd. Aren't I funny looking? "

"Granddad!"

"Ok, well, you see yourself differently than if you're looking in a mirror. Anyhow, I just floated away; it was your Dad's power, strength whatever that grounded me in that garden."

"So he stopped you floating into space?"

"I think so; I think I annoyed him a bit, just floating about all over playing with it. So he stopped me in the garden with the fancy bushes, then said we had a job to do."

"Do you think the garden is heaven?"

"No, definitely not, it's just a meeting place. A base. Nice though. Reminded me of Chatsworth house, remember when we had a day out there, and a picnic by the pond, gosh, you were a right scruffy little thing."

"Grandad".

"Well, when we finished with the dog, your Dad gave me a gentle nudge, and here I am, ringing you."

"What happened to the dog?"

"The dog was imaginary chicken."

"Yes, yes, I know, oh it doesn't matter."

"I don't know if you've noticed, but the dog was actually Jet, your best pal when you were a little girl. You loved that dog."

"Why show me him like that?"

"I think it's to show that people are not nasty on the outside, it's on the inside. To be on your guard. Wolf in sheep's clothing and all that."

"Ah. So, did we discuss why you wouldn't do it again?"

"Well. I was attached to my body by a string. A life line. Without anyone telling me, I knew, if the string broke, I'd be dead."

"It didn't though, so it must be strong."

"Only because your Dad was there, I can't guarantee that next time, no. I've had enough, I'll wait until my numbers up."

"So what now?"

"You fight."

I spend the rest of the day thinking about the dream and what Granddad has said. Fight? Fight what? The rude customers? The ignorant advertising men?

By three o'clock, I begin to make changes, I write a letter to the advertising company cancelling my agreement and demanding my initial cheque back. I ring my bank and cancel the cheque, and subsequent direct debits.

I make a notice detailing terms and conditions of refunds.

I serve Dave with an eviction notice. Not legal, but it will be, if he doesn't comply.

I leave the van alone. Mums right it's family after all. At least it's still in the family. I was being a little too bitter about that I think.

I'm laminating a No FOOD, DRINK or WET Umbrellas sign when the phone rings.

Michelle. "My Louis doesn't want to go boxing tonight."

I find myself a little disappointed. I wasn't looking forward to dragging myself there either, but knowing I had to, as part of a promise, well, it was planned now. Mum was having Mickey this time, save him staying up late. I'd become used to the release over the past few months.

"Why not?"

"The trainer's, he says they were nasty to him. They said if he wasn't going to punch properly he may as well stay at home."

I remember this bit, Lenny and Tommy doing their usual good cop, bad cop. I'm surprised though, tough Louis, giving in over a tiny bit of criticism.

"Surely he should try one more time, he can't just give up, he can't."

"Well, he is, so you're off the hook. No need to take him anymore. Catch you later, bye."

That's it. Phone dead. Oh well.

Maybe not.

A whisper begins in my head, "fight, fight, fight, fight," I make the decision, there and then, I'm not going to give up at the first hurdle either. Just because there's no one holding my hand, doesn't mean I have to stop going.

I've a key to my own private dressing room for heaven's sake.

Just a flash of the boxing club and walking in alone, fills me with a nervous anticipation that sees a beads of perspiration instantly form on my top lip. I know I have to do this. This is what Dad was talking about, this is my fight, in the most literal sense of the word.

Chapter 16

I'm so nervous, as I park the car and take the long cold walk to the boxing club alone. I've bought my own wraps, long red bandages that have a hook over the thumb, and Velcro to secure in place. My knuckles have hardly recovered from the last time. I'm also prepared with bottles of water and a towel for the perspiration, all kept snugly in a sports shoulder bag. I didn't think my fake Chanel handbag would be appreciated here.

I haven't bought gloves, as I don't want to seem arrogant, besides, there are so many different ounces, I wouldn't know where to start and would only make a fool of myself. It wasn't until I had a little look whilst buying the wraps, did I notice that the ones I'd used on the Monday were bag gloves. Useless for fighting with.

A few well seasoned amateur boxer jog past me on the way up the hill to the portacabin. The track is covered in weeds, and the garden outside the cabin a wasteland. A dumping ground for the local residents. There's a fair bit of empty space, but the rest has old washing machines, broken fences, smashed glass, and goodness knows what else hidden in the shrubbery border. The cast iron gates are open to all of this and the boxing club as a whole.

Night has fallen, and the light from a crack in the door shines out. My mind wants to run away, I want to bolt, yet I know this is what Dad was aiming for. For me to step out of my comfort zone, to challenge myself, to reach my full potential, and to ultimately stop being scared.

I open the door to nothing, not the murmurs I was expecting, or the deathly silence I'd imagined. Everyone carries on as if I hadn't entered at all. About twenty boys and men are stretching just right of the ring. I dump my bag on one of the spectator's chairs, and move to the hatch to pay Tommy my subs.

"Where's your lad?" His first question.

"With my mum, why, is he allowed here?" I think this would make it a lot easier knowing he was, instead of calling on favours.

"Never too young to learn a bit of the technique. Ok, what do you owe me, how many of you tonight?"

"Just me."

He looks at me a little quizzically, as if deciding whether to tell me to go home or not, yet he says nothing.

"You're brave. They'll make mincemeat out of you."

I shrug, as my voice would betray my nerves. I keep my eye on the door, contemplating making a break for it. Once I reached the safety of my car, I need never come back, I could go home.

I could go home and be scared or I could stay and fight.

As I begin to put on my wraps, I nod to one of the mothers sat on a chair next to my bag. She's become a familiar face since that first time, tonight I'm too nervous to make small talk.

"I'm rooting for you!" She smiles.

This warms my heart, "really, why, thank you, it's not easy, getting up there."

"No, I can see that, but just by doing it, I think you've got bigger balls than the rest of them."

If she could feel me shivering inside, she wouldn't think so.

"Anyway," she continues, "don't let me keep you, you've work to do, I couldn't take my eyes off you last time."

Oh dear, "I'm not, you know, I'm really very feminine out of here, it's just, well easier to dress like a boy for boxing."

She laughs and slaps her thigh; I notice she's about twenty years older than me, with a gold tooth, and bitten nails.

"Me too, love, me too. I've a hubby at home, no doubt moaning because his diner isn't on table, I'm not that way either. I've always liked boxing though, my son, my Callum," she points to a teenage boy punching a black bag, "he's a natural, and watching you, I think you might be too."

I shake my head, I like books, Egyptian cotton, fresh flowers and baking bread, I'm not a boxer, no way. She takes my left hand and tightens the wrap around it. I wince a little, but have complete trust that she knows better than me how to put these on.

"I don't think so, I'm not the type. Thank you though. I'm here for fitness, that's all. Tommy and Lenny seem to have forgotten that."

"John will forget that too, as soon as he sees you, you haven't met him yet."

"Who is he?"

"He's in the changing room right now, he's the founder of the club."

"I thought Tommy was the owner?"

"No, he's a retired boxer, just a trainer, fantastic though."

"Lenny?"

"Lenny's the same, he tours with Paul Ingle, and he's well respected, this little club's lucky to have them. Paul's been coming here since he was ten; he grew up on the council estate."

She slaps my hands to show she's finished, my hands feel squashed, and tight, I want to free my little finger it's almost claustrophobic. I clench and unclench my fists to loosen the wraps a little, as I walk to the others warming up. Nobody says hello. A few nod but don't make eye contact. There's no gossiping between them. My heart is beating madly and a flush is creeping up my face. I lower my eyes, not my head, and copy Lenny who's warming up in the centre.

"Tiptoes," he orders, and winks at me.

"Jogging on the spot," I follow his lead and start. After just one minute, my breathing becomes heavier, I'm prepared, as I know last time, we had a huge run after this, my heart is beating furiously, and already I need water. A mixture of nerves and anticipation.

"And GO!" He sweeps his arm around the gym. The boys and men set off at a furious pace. I try to keep up. My tracksuit bottoms keep falling down, and as I run I pull them up, worried about revealing my flabby tummy, or underwear.

"PUNCH UP!" Who would have thought it would be so much hard work just to raise our arms whilst running?

"DROP, give me twenty!" With a thud, and no questions we do, all of us. Through the familiar beads of sweat, I see a new man talking to Lenny in the centre of the room. He's about ten years older than me, dark, bright blue eyes, and a thoughtful face. He's nodding as Lenny's chatting to him. As we start running again, I can hardly take my eyes off him. His nose has been broken before, I can see that. He's not gorgeous, but he has a certain presence.

Lenny hasn't barked an order for two minutes; he's so engrossed in his gossip mongering.

"HOP!" shouts the new man. So we do. It was as easy as a child, now, it seems not one of us can hop for more than five steps. We all laugh a little as the slow runners pass the fast ones, and we stop ourselves falling over each other. As Lenny carries on talking oblivious, the new man smirks when we all end up in a tangled heap on top of each other near the doors.

The new man, who I decide must be John, starts helping us all up; he grabs my hand but doesn't look me in the eye. I'm steady on my feet when he pats my back, "come on, all of you outside, PT now!" His pat turns into a shove towards the door as I follow the rest outside.

We jog down the hill towards the main road and the shops, the pavements are as busy as are the roads. I'm grateful it's dark,-hopefully I won't be recognised. We take a route through the houses, and then up a hill through a newly built housing estate. My throat feels red raw, I'm certain my little toes are bleeding, and I dare not cough in case I vomit. I have a stitch; I'm considering the consequences of just stopping, right here, and now, when John jogs effortlessly beside me for a minute. My mouth is unattractively wide open, as if I'm catching flies, in reality it's my body's way of absorbing all available oxygen. With the cold hitting my hot face, it seems as though I'm drooling a little. There is absolutely no way I would be able to speak right now.

He jogs alongside me for a little while, looking me up and down as if weighing up each footfall and wobble. Without a word, when we reach the top of the hill he speeds off.

I can see the boxing club, my bones are rattling with each pound on the ground. I'm resisting every urge to drop to all fours and crawl through the door. I need water, I need to stop, my chest is about to explode, every limb burns with an intense heat, and each bang on the ground intensifies a migraine that is threatening to erupt.

Tommy is stood at the door; he shakes his head as I veer off the straight path and head for him through the cast iron gates.

"There are another five laps yet lady." He smirks.

I've no chance; I have to give up, right now. I nearly cry.

With the light from the club behind him, his nose touching the darkness outside, Lenny looks like my guardian angel, as he speaks up for me.

"Don't you remember your first time Tommy? Give the lass a break eh?"

He moves aside so I can pass him into the gym, "go on, go get a drink, and don't stop though. Whatever you do, don't stop, keep walking."

I take his advice; it seems my body doesn't want to stop, not yet. I pick up my water as Callum's mum shakes her head at me, on my second lap of the gym; I reach past her for a skipping rope.

"Just what have you got to prove?" She asks curiously.

"I've got to prove I'm worthy of my life. That I'm not a shirker, that I can protect my son, I can take care of my mum; I have a hell of a lot to prove."

"That's some burden for a young girls shoulder,"

"Yeah, but I don't see anyone else stepping up, do you?"

"Maybe because they think you have all the angles covered, they've no need to?"

I nod, she has a point, and I can't stop now. Whilst every part of me screamed in agony whilst running outside, there was one psychological part that was as light as a feather, empty and ready to fly. My mind.

So much did I concentrate on keeping upright, steadying my breathing, I had no space for anything else, and it felt good. I felt good. I had a purpose; I had something, totally, all for me. I was being quite selfish whilst proving this point.

I take a couple of strong painkillers I'd become used to with my migraines.

My migraines being a fact of live from as early as I can remember; I always found prevention much easier than a cure.

"Not surprised you have headache, it's freezing out there," mutters Callum's mum, she pats my elbow, and "I'm Vicky by the way."

"Tina," I gulp. Tommy shouts across the gym as little by little other boxers begin filling up the empty space, the full six laps over for them.

"We don't have time to chat, if you want to train here, you will TRAIN here. You DON'T get to pick and choose."

He walks up to me, determination in his eyes; I've already made a half-hearted attempt to start skipping. I'm useless at skipping.

He lowers his voice so no one can hear him but me; to my surprise, his words are almost kind.

"You are taking the piss lady do you think I will waste my time training a smoker. I will not! Don't deny it."

"I won't, I'll stop." I'd actually been weaning myself off for quite some time, more for Mickey's benefit than my own; however Dad's clogged arteries had sent me spinning to the chemist only a few days before, where I swiftly spent a small fortune on patches.

"The other thing,"

"Yes?"

"You're too fat. You need to lose weight. At least a stone. If we are to get you match fit, you need to lose that belly of yours."

He's not said anything I've not thought myself. I nod, as he shocks me with an announcement, "I've lined you up for a fight, a real fight. Featherweight. It's a pretty important place to start, in a city, against a well seasoned girl. I watched her fight last week, and she's good."

My life almost flashes before my eyes.

"I've no chance, it's been ten sessions only, I have absolutely no chance of fighting, I wouldn't know how."

"NO, but in six weeks time you will, you are my new challenge, and boy do I need one."

I feel giddy, excited and sick all at once. I'm proud of myself, I'm proud that he feels I'm worthy of his time and effort. I'm proud that he's seen some talent in me.

Returning home that evening, I turn the key in the lock to find mum, sat on the floor in front of a real log fire. Still in night clothes, but the change of position is pleasing. On the floor is an arrangement of cards. Tarot cards.

She is smiling, she's happy, whatever they are telling her, it must be good.

"I've the three of swords in my past that means destitution, heart break, unspeakable loss."

I sit in Dad's chair and perch on the edge as I watch.

"The five of wands in my future means I have got to let someone or something go on their journey, I'm not to hold them back."

"Ok, that's Dad is it?"

"No, I think it might be you, I don't know why, anyhow, the present, I got the nine of swords, that's the worst card you can get."

Mum couldn't be in a much worse place realistically. Quite impressive.

"The ace of cups though, combined with the star, means my future is bright. Someone will want and need my love. Wholly. Completely, and it will be my mission in life to love them."

"I thought Dad was the love of your life."

"He was, gosh, he so was, he still is, I can't imagine that either. I did yours earlier, hope you don't mind?"

"No. I'm not sure I believe it if I'm honest."

"Well, I did them straight after I got a phone call. You got the ace of everything, cups, coins, wands, swords that means every area of your life will be new. EVERY area."

"The phone call mum, who was it?"

Mum looks a little sheepish, but there's a twinkle in her eye.

"Mickey's Dad darling."

Well, knock me down with a featherweight.

Chapter 17

I pick up the phone to dial the number mum has scribbled down on the pad next to it. Mum's still flicking backwards and forwards through her tarot book, checking the cards before flicking again. She looks at peace a little; it almost feels as though it's mum again, but not quite.

I'm still exhausted, yet when Harry answers the phone, my adrenalin starts pumping all over for a second time. I nearly hang up, I've not thought this through. It's been two and a half years.

"It's Tina, Harry."

He clears his throat; I can hear a smile in voice when he answers.

"Blimey, gosh, I didn't know if you would get back to me, you could have ignored me, but thank you."

"Thank me?"

"Well, yes, little understated I guess. You've brought up my son alone for nearly three years and all I can say is Thank you. Even I know you deserve a hell of a lot more than that."

His humble attitude is confusing me. I have never come close to hating Harry, after everything, I understand, and know he has a good heart somewhere, but I have added a little arrogance to his personality over the last few years.

"So, what's up Harry?" I'm not comfortable with this conversation, and I don't like his choice of words. My son?

"I saw in the paper about your Dad. I'm so sorry. He was a fantastic man, one of a kind."

"I know".

"I bet Mickey misses him."

"Yes he does. We all do. It's a blow, a hell of a blow."

"I'd like to make it a little easier if you'll let me?"

"Go on."

"Have you a boyfriend at the moment?"

"Not that it's any of your business, but no. No, I don't think Mickey needs mummy dating on top of the stress of losing his Grandad."

"Phew. I was worried it would be all complicated and messy. Now, it should be quite simple."

"What should?"

His voice has completely lost its smile when he answers , "I want custody of Mickey Tina."

Just like that the blood leaves my head. I can feel it draining, from my head to my toes. Each body part becoming weaker and colder by the second. I put the phone back on the hook, and sit on Dad's chair. My arms as heavy as lead, I will my body to move. I need to be with Mickey. Just to have him close, to know he's here.

Mum eyes me suspiciously.

"I don't think that boxing is doing you any good." I can't even say out loud the words Harry has just spoken to me. This would send mum over the edge. Maybe if I ignore it, it will go away.

"They want me to fight, they say I have talent." No answer, so I try to appeal to mums basic instinct, "I could make a lot of money at it."

Mum shakes her head and returns to her cards. "Don't be so ridiculous. You're not a boxer."

"Apparently I am".

"Well you're bloody stupid if you ask me, broken bones, for what?"

"It makes me feel good."

"Find a different hobby."

"It's not a hobby, it's real. It's only self-defence after all. The most primitive form of self defence."

"It's bloody selfish is what it is. What about Mickey?"

"I'm doing it for Mickey."

"Oh yes, he'll be so happy watching his mother get a beating."

"If I train hard enough I won't, that's the point."

"Suit yourself."

So I do. Without eating, drinking, without another daily action, I take myself up to bed, to Mickey. To the ten foot square room, one of the only places where I feel my life and family is my own.

The next morning is a day off. The sun is shining betraying the cold air, I feel heavy with decisions. I'm confused, and can't work out what is best. I don't know if I'm being selfish or sensible. There's only one person who will help me through it. Grandma.

Before Grandma, Dad would have been the first choice. He would have solved my dilemmas with a few wise words, made it simple. Removed the complications, yet he's not here. Grandma is a good substitute. She loves me, that's all that matters.

I know we will be all day if we visit, so I pack Mickey a lunch, leave mum with Jane and set off on our merry way. Just leaving the house makes my heart lighter. My shoulders lift, and a sense of pride infiltrates once again. I start singing with Mickey. He's in his seat at the front, always seems silly having him so far out of reach, I've had the airbag at his side removed especially. He's smiling and chuckling. We're chatting about nothing. It's so light, so heart warming I can't help but feel a little guilty for being cheerful again.

The forty mile journey seems to take seconds, and before long I'm stood in front of Gran's kettle whilst Mickey pulls out all the toys she's hand made for him.

"It's lovely to see you Tinsey, so good".

Gran's second husband David walks through from the bedroom, he squeezes me tight, and holds on for dear life. I have to remove his hands to free myself.

"My page three girl, how you doing?" he asks.

I shrug.

"See, I knew it," says Gran, "it is lovely to see you, but I knew as soon as you walked through that door, that it's because you have a problem. It's not just losing your Dad either is it?"

I shake my head, and to my surprise a tear falls, just one. I try to suck it back in, I can't cry, not now. Not here.

"David," Gran orders, "make the coffees, Tina, come sit. Tell me. Let's put the telly on for Mickey, so he can't hear, yeah?"

I nod. When I hear the deep sing song voice of Barney I begin.

"Mum wants me to give up boxing." I blurt.

"OK, solvable, I didn't know you'd started. You can't blame her though?"

"No, no I can't, but she doesn't get it. Since Dad died, nothings felt safe anymore. Nothing. Everything's so insecure. I feel as if I will lose what I have left any second. Not only that, I don't feel protected. We're unsafe too. There's no one to look after us. Boxing helps. It really helps."

"How?" A feeling of self-indulgence overcomes me. I've not had this much attention since Dad was alive and well. It's surprising me that someone is taking the time to ask, and looks interested to know the answer.

"I feel as though I'm not made of glass. Every little cut reminds me that I'm alive, and my body can take much more than I give it credit for. It tells me I should fear dying, because I have every right to survive."

"Are you scared of dying?"

"No, I'm scared of leaving Mickey behind."

Gran nods. "So is that it. It makes you feel alive?"

"Well, that's enough but no. It makes me feel as though I'm doing my best to protect my family. After just ten sessions, I feel more confident. I know I'd stand a better chance against an attacker. A chance that gets better every time I train."

"That's not your job though Tinsey, is it?" Gran lowers her voice sympathetically. It's almost too much to take. I take a deep breath to stop the tears that are threatening to flow.

"I don't see anyone else stepping up Gran?"

"No neither do I love, neither do I. You keep at it. You're not stupid; you won't let it become a risk to your life. If it's doing all that, it must be ok."

I feel better already and not selfish at all. Dare I confess the phone call? I check on Mickey, and see him engrossed in the television, whilst David tries to play bingo with him. Confident that he can't hear me, I confess.

"Mickey's dad rang last night."

Gran smiles, she has always wanted me to settle down. Finding love twice in her life, she hates to see others go without.

"Wants to see Mickey I suppose?" She asks.

"Wants to take him off me more like."

Gran runs her finger through her short curly grey hair. She takes off her glasses, letting them hang round her neck, then she rubs her eyes. She too makes sure Mickey's not listening.

"FULL custody, are you sure?"

"Uh - huh."

Gran sweeps off imaginary dirt on her arms with her hands, sits up straight, then declares,

"Well the fellows a barmy pot. Mental. He really thinks he'll win does he?"

"He sounded pretty confident to me."

"No rings, no rights."

"Pardon?"

"In Woman magazine last month, they had a story about unmarried fathers. Says they have a huge task trying to gain even supervised visits when there's not been any legal binding involved. Is Harry on the birth certificate?"

"No, awful it was, I had to register Mickey as father unknown as Harry was touring Europe on the day of registration."

"He's no chance. He's got to have a DNA test first. What exactly did he say on the telephone?"

I tell her all of it. She starts laughing and shakes her head.

"Tina, I sometimes wish you wouldn't be so impulsive, who knows what he would have said next. He may be asking for partial custody. Every second weekend?"

"I didn't think if that. I just thought it's my luck. I was losing my boy."

"Well, first thing I think you should do is get yourself a solicitor, then you're prepared when he rings again."

"You think he'll ring again."

"Of course he will. Problems don't just disappear because you put the phone down."

She's right, I know. I stand up to fill the kettle, one last cuppa then home. David has opened Mickey's lunch for him, and is growling at Mickey's command.

"Right now you're sorted, I'd like you to do something for me. Well to answer a question really."

"Ok, anything Gran, go on."

"Well you said you weren't afraid of dying, why is that?"

"You'll think I'm crazy if I tell you Gran."

"No change there then. Try me. Go on, it's important."

"Well, I've always seen things. Anyway since Dad died, I've seen more. Dreams mainly, but dreams that make sense. I wouldn't have coped without them."

"So you truly believe there's life after death?"

"I do yes. Definitely. If not, then the mind is an absolutely wonderful phenomenon, but it brings the images from somewhere. If the mind is so great as to show me ghosts, give me dreams, give me my father for a few hours, then surely it's great enough to live on?"

"You make a lot of sense. So you're 100% sure in your heart?"

"Yes Gran, why?"

"Because I'm dying, and I think I need your help."

Chapter 18

"Don't be so silly Gran, you'll be around forever you will. Like a creaking gate!"

As I say it, I know it's not true. No one ever imagined Gran to live this long. Emphysema, osteoporosis, a medley of terrible conditions sees Gran dependant on oxygen and electric wheelchairs. With every hospital visit, the full family fear the worst.

Somehow, this blow does not hit as hard as it may have done before Dad's death. Far from doubling the pain, it seems to numb instead. As if all of my grief receptors have been used up mourning Dad. I have no reserves left, no matter how much I love the person.

Gran being still alive may help too.

"Look, you know I wouldn't say it if I didn't mean it, you're the only one I can talk to. Everyone else thinks I'm batty."

"You are Gran." I joke.

"Oi."

"Ok, why do you think your number is up? You do know, if you die, mum may not cope at all."

"Your mum will cope, I'm sure of that."

"You can't be Gran. She's not handling this one too well, anything else, well it doesn't bear thinking about. Besides I'm pretty partial to you myself."

"Your mum will cope, because she has you. I know my time is coming. I know because I met your Dad, in the garden."

"This garden?"

"No, you know which garden. I met him. I asked if my time was close, he nodded. He's always tolerated me your father, mind I didn't make life easy for him to start with. I just thought he was a cockney rebel."

"At the age he met mum Gran, he probably was."

I'm a little perturbed that Gran has seen the garden. Both Gran and Granddad now. It makes me wonder if there's a whole congregation of old people who keep these little secrets to themselves, or indeed don't realise that the pleasant dreams are actually preparation for the next step. Death. It makes me want to start a personal advert.

"Do you have dreams about a garden full of bushes? Do you hear running water? Are you young and free? Maybe lost? Do NOT panic....meet us at the bookshop, we have some life changing news to impart."

We could call it the "Nearly There Club".

One foot in the grave even more than apt. One foot in God's Garden more literal.

I bring myself back to the present as Gran takes out paperwork from a pocket of her electric wheelchair.

"Right," she says, "I didn't want to leave all this up to you lot, so I've started to arrange my own funeral. Did you know if I wanted you all to perform cartwheels around my grave, all I have to do is write it in this little folder?"

"I'd probably fall in your grave Gran if I tried that!"

"Yes, you probably would. You'd be the only one daft enough to give it a go too. No I've not gone that far, but I have requested that nobody wears black."

"Black is so slimming though Gran, I love black."

"Have a pink flower or something then."

I shake my head, stand up and pace the tiny kitchen a little. I've just lost my father, my mum's on holiday mentally, and now, I'm planning my Grandmother's funeral whilst she's still alive.

It doesn't stress me or upset me, yet it seems a little surreal.

"It's all done," she reassures me. "I just need you to listen to me. To not call me mad for thinking this will happen. To talk through everything, my choices, the future. Seeing how you've dealt with this has shown me how strong you are. You are your mum's best friend Tinsey, and she yours, though you may not see it right now. You're also mine. You're the only person I can talk to."

"You do a fair bit of listening yourself Gran."

"Then we'll help each other, I just want my passing to be a pleasant as possible."

I look at David, muttering away to Mickey, and feel a wave of sadness. If this is true, he soon will feel what mum is feeling.

I nod, "does he know Gran?"

Gran looks surprised, "who? David? Why yes, of course he does. He doesn't believe it though. Thinks it's another phase I'm going through, but he's humouring me."

I feel a little relief, and an emotion I didn't expect. Jealousy. Silence descends on the kitchen, I fill the kettle whilst staring out of the window, the weather, the dark meaningless, and I realise I'm jealous of David.

Jealous because he knows, he has a chance to say goodbye. He has a chance to right every wrong, to erase any doubt of his love in my grandmother's mind. He has all of that. When Gran does die, he can grieve knowing he did all he could, that she died knowing she was one in a million, that there will never be another. Never.

Dad died knowing nothing of the sort.

I physically shake hoping to rid myself of this ugly thought. It would now not change a thing, I should be happy that David has this chance, not bitter.

"So are you ill Gran?" I ask, trying to find some logical reason to this funeral planning.

"No more than usual. I think it will be quick, when it happens, it will be quick."

"When, when do you think it will happen?" I have a mind full of questions. I believe her, yet I don't want to.

"I've a good month left yet, I'm sure of it, but I'll rest knowing everything's done."

"What would you like me to do?"

"Well, " she begins, "I've prepared a system. To save fighting. I've seen how even strangers are begging your mum for your fathers precious possessions, so I have divided everything the way I want it to go."

"In your Will?"

"Nope, with stickers. Everyone has a colour, you for example are blue. You like blue. Your mum is yellow and so on. Everything I'm leaving has a sticker on, if it's your colour, it's yours. I'm in half a mind to let people come and get it now, it'd be such fun seeing everyone clambering looking for their colour.

Mickey is purple by the way."

I have an overwhelming urge to look. A strong curiosity. I appreciate from experience that this will be part of Gran's game. She will enjoy this, watching to see how everyone reacts. See how greedy they are.

I don't think of myself as being greedy, wanting to know. After all, I want for nothing material, I have everything I need, yet I do feel as though I would like to see what Gran thinks of me. It's not long before I have my answer.

"If you're wondering, I will give you a hint. My material, my gadgets. I leave to you."

This makes perfect sense. I've always coveted Gran's gadgets. Her unhealthy obsession with television shopping giving her every kitchen accessory a budding Delia would want.

She continues to explain, "See I can see you're happy with that, whereas others wouldn't be."

"Why ever not?" I ask.

"Second hand material, second hand gadgets, they're not worth a lot are they?"

"They are to me Gran, every time I bake a loaf of bread I'll think of you."

"Exactly, and that's what I've hoped to do. I really hope I've given everyone something they will use a lot, and think of me whilst they do."

"Well you got me right, I'm sure you will everyone else."

"Yeah, I think so. Aunty Sue likes clocks, your mum loves earrings. Mickey loves my solitaire, and bingo. Yep, I think I've done ok."

"So what else would you like me to do Gran?"

"There's a song, I want it playing at the funeral. I don't know who it's by though; will you find it for me?"

Gran takes my hand and starts rocking it gently. *"Place your hand in my hand as we walk across the water,"* she sings. I commit it to memory whilst she finishes the words she knows.

"So what are you going to do now?" asks Gran.

"Go home, cook dinner, and go boxing." I reply, thinking it's obvious. Existing rather than living at the moment.

"What about Harry? Are you going to run away, or ring him back?"

"What's the point of ringing him back? He may completely forget about it, then I've just reminded him. No, I'll leave it be." I start to walk towards Mickey, if I'm going to make it to boxing I need to get my skates on.

"But if you ring first," Gran says to my back," then you have the upper hand, that must be better than him catching you unawares. He won't go away you know."

I think she may be right. With a sleepy Mickey nestled on my right hip I lean in to give Gran a cuddle. David rubs me on the shoulder.

"I'll see you soon, very soon. Don't go anywhere in the meantime, ok?"

Gran laughs, a light laugh. As I walk away, I cannot help but think that funeral planning must be good for the soul, on some level.

On our return home, I walk into the house with trepidation. Mum says nothing to start with. I plan on feeding Mickey then taking him with me to boxing. I'm sure with snacks and a colouring book he'll be just fine on the sidelines.

It seems mum reads my mind.

"I'm sorry," she whispers.

"What for?" I ask.

"For yesterday, there were better ways of handling it. I don't like it; I don't want to lose you too."

"You're not losing my mum. It's a hobby, nothing more."

"I feel like I am. If I stop you, if I try, it will only make you more determined. I know that. I was scared. I'm sorry."

"I'm not going to stop the boxing mum. Not until I've had enough. If I can't fight the inevitable, at least give me a chance at being able to fight the tangible?"

"I understand, I don't like it, but I understand."

I feel relief. I've missed my mum. Everything she is seemed to have died with Dad, yet it's a relief to know she can come back, even if Dad can't. With mum about, I can tackle anything.

"There's a parcel there," she says pointing to a brown paper package. "I think it's the gloves you ordered."

I open it to reveal two black, ten ounce fighting gloves. Not bag gloves, real bona fide fighting gloves. They smell new and not of sweaty feet like the ones at the club do.

"Thanks mum. I'm just going to get Mickey some dinner, then we're off." I say.

"You're taking Mickey with you? To boxing, tonight?"

I nod, "please mum, don't start, I have to do this. I don't know why."

"No, no, you don't understand, I'll have Mickey. He shouldn't have to see you fighting. I'll look after him, anytime you want to go."

Fantastic.

"Thank you. In that case, I have just enough time to make one phone call before I leave."

Chapter 19

Passing Mickey to mum, I change quickly, then curl up on Dad's chair to use the telephone. I already have adrenalin coursing through my veins at the thought of this evenings boxing, yet as I lift the receiver my heart pounds and my mouth dries.

Mum is playing with Mickey about four feet away in front of the fire. She doesn't know what Harry said the other night, absolutely no idea. She looks at me strangely, as I'm hesitating with the receiver in my hand.

I scroll through the received calls list and hit the green button when I see the only one that's not familiar. It must be his.

He answers after the third ring.

I smile reassuringly at mum and walk into the kitchen. My heart is pounding.

"Harry." I say, trying to sound confident, glad he's not in front of me to see me trembling. "It's Tina, I'm sorry for hanging up the other night. It seems I got the wrong end of the stick."

He thinks for a second before replying. "Wrong end of the stick? I don't blame you for hanging up, I wasn't very tactful. Maybe this would be easier face to face."

I stride across the kitchen and close the door. I don't want to risk Mickey or Mum hearing the conversation.

"With Mickey." He adds as an afterthought.

No. No way. Absolutely not. No. Mickey does not need this. Mickey is coping extremely well. Mickey needs stability, and I need to see if this man, this man who legged it, who left us without a goodbye, I need to see if he's changed. If he can be the father he should be.

Until then, no Mickey. No mum either. I can see it now, mum becoming excited, then worried, then anxious, then scared. I need to do this alone, and soon before another sleepless night.

I pick the perfect place. The place I feel most secure, at my strongest, my decision is quick, and I'm relieved. "I'll be at the boxing club on Chapel Street; you can see me for half an hour when I've finished. About eight o'clock. Tonight."

I'm expecting questions, I get none. "Fine." He says, and then it's his turn to hang up.

I tell mum I'll be home a little later than usual, hug Mickey, and leave. My minds a blur, but I'm heading towards the perfect place. I need to rid myself of nervous energy, of anger, of tears even, the boxing club will let me do this without asking questions.

I'm ten minutes late by the time I'm walking up the hill towards the portacabin. I'm in a daze and can barely remember my journey at all.

I enter to shouting and hollering. Then I realise it's directed at me.

"Come on!" Shouts Lenny. He's stood in the middle of a circle of male boxers. They all cheer with him. "We thought we'd put you off, come on!"

I quickly drop my bag with Callums' mum and join them all.

"Finally," says John to my right, "the gangs all here."

They don't know it, but they have just saved me from entering a dark place. I was sinking fast, letting bitterness creep in. I was an hour away from a victims cry of, "Why me?" At my lowest ebb, these have shown me there is kindness, I do fit in, I am doing what's best. I am. I break away before the run to drink water and take my painkillers, and then I'm back and I watch John's pert bum lead us round the gym.

The fast air hits my wet face. I'd started with the silent tears over five minutes ago, but if anyone noticed they didn't let on. That's the great thing about this boxing club, about mixing with males only. They don't feel the need to know every detail. They have no idea of my story; they just know that I am a woman who has a drive inside her willing her to box. I'm just like them only a different gender.

All three trainers are here today, Lenny, Tommy and John. There's also a man I don't recognise. He's punching a bag whilst the rest of us run around the gym. His gloves are brand new and he-has sunglasses resting on the top of his bald head. With every strike he grunts, loudly, so I cannot help but look. He is drawing attention to himself, acting like a prat in my opinion, yet the boys and trainers seem to be ok with it. I know, if it were me distracting everyone like that, I'd be in for a showdown. I carry on regardless, and let my mind free itself as I run outside. The cold air yet again sucks the breath from my body but instead of stopping to catch it I carry on. At a steady pace I pass the pain barrier, past the point where I think I am going to pass out. I pass it all. I pass my personal best then call it quits.

John gives me thumbs up and winks as he sees me jog back towards the club. I grab my water without breaking step past the spectator's seats. Striding quickly, then slower, I see the mystery man has not broken a sweat, yet is still making the same noise.

He stops. "Come here." He orders. I carry on, he cannot be talking to me, I don't know the man. Lenny is placing old gloves in pairs on a dusty table in the far corner. His ears prick up. I carry on walking.

"Come. Here." The mystery man points at me this time.

As I pass Lenny he whispers, almost a growl, "just do as he says, I'll explain later."

I trust Lenny so I do.

"I'm Simon," the man removes a glove, there are no wraps on his hands, but he offers one for me to shake. I do.

"I've heard a lot about you," he goes on. I notice he talks as if he's the most important person in the room. He's not. Not in my eyes anyhow. "So let's see if the rumours are justified. Put your gloves on. Come with me."

I take my wraps and gloves, and follow; I'm unrolling one wrap, letting it uncoil until it hits the floor, when he stops me.

"You don't need those on."

I speak to him for the first time. "I do, my knuckles, they graze on the fabric of the gloves, it kills."

He nods to my gloves. "First of all, if you are going to learn anything you need to listen and not argue ok?" Without pausing he carries on." Those are new gloves are they not?"

I look to John as he walks in from the run. He shrugs his shoulders then makes his way over to Lenny.

"Yes, I've not worn them yet."

"Then they'll be YOUR gloves. No one else's. Do NOT let anyone else wear those gloves. They will mould to your hands, they will know your hands, they will feel like silk mittens by the time we've finished, not ten-ounce gloves. You understand?"

Even if I didn't I wouldn't argue. I take off another layer of clothes, revealing a boxers baggy vest underneath. I'm long past vanity. Vanity has no place in this club. Not whilst training anyhow.

John walks over and takes one of the spectator's seats next to us; looking on with curiosity.

"I don't think you should be doing this Simon. Tina's a bit different to the boys you know." Says John.

Simon blusters. His chest puffs out, imitating a robin red breast. His sunglasses nearly wobble, and for the first time I see beads of perspiration on his bald head. I try not to smile. He's comical. He's also incredulous. "Look Johnny," he spits.

"John actually." Says John without raising his voice at all.

"Whatever. I have heard about this girl, woman, boxer. She wants to be treated the same as the boys, so she will be treated exactly the same ok?"

John starts to argue but I interrupt.

"It's fine. Really, it's fine. He's right. I don't want any special treatment."

Simon smirks. He's won. I've played right into his hands.

John stands up to walk away, shaking his head. "Well don't expect me to stand and watch. Make it quick Simon, if nothing else."

Once out of earshot Simon picks up some red and black leather pads. He places them on his own hands.

"I am going to introduce you to power and combinations. A bloody good cocktail. You ready? Come on."

He holds the pads up then bounces about using his calves. I'm not used to this. I'm used to a bag that stays still. I take half my weight off the floor, yet make sure my back foot stays solid. He starts barking in my ear.

"Left. Right. Left." Slowly at first. He's smirking again. I'm hitting the pads but not with enough power. I'm putting all of my concentration into seeing him, expecting the next one. He raises the pads, then hides them, turns around, expecting me to follow. I do. He becomes faster.

He shouts above the noise of the others skipping. They've all returned, and the slap of rope and wire hitting bare floorboards drowns out almost everything else.

"I'm not going to warn you now. I'm just going to twitch. You have to see this and hit. If I shout left and right, I mean your hand. You have to get used to starting combinations with your opposite hand."

I start to argue. Being naturally right handed, Tommy has had me starting with my left anyhow, to build strength. So to defy this and use the one that's normal for me seems silly.

"You're a South Paw right?" He shouts.

"No." I answer. It's true I'm not.

"Well, you fooled me. Come on!" I rise a few inches hearing this. This tiny scrap of encouragement, this backhanded obscure compliment fills me with pride. I have talent. I actually have a talent.

Another four minutes of hitting the bags like a robot and I zone out. The ringside bell fades, I don't hear the rounds, and the skipping ropes disappear. All I see are the pads. It becomes instinct to hit the one which flinches towards me. Simon's sunglasses are still on the top of his head, I take a look and remember Tommy's advice to use my shoulder, push the weight forward and then snap. I miss a jab from Simon but catch up as I put Tommy's advice to practice. Simon loses his footing, his legs bend, yet as he tries to straighten up his sunglasses wobble, then crash and smash onto the bare floor.

The full gym erupts in applause.

Simon picks up what he can of his glasses, as Lenny comes over with a dust pan and brush.

"She did good Simon, didn't she?" provokes Lenny.

Simon nods as he paces away.

I bend down to whisper to Lenny on the floor.

"Come on then Len, who is he?"

"He's the money Shorty. He owns this club. Without his cash we can't exist. He knows hardly anything about boxing, but we have to keep him on side. None of us have the funds to spare to keep it going. It doesn't make money you see. Just swallows it."

I understand. Completely.

We stand up together, the conspirator whispers gone.

"Go find John, tell him you've not taken your gloves off yet."

I'm perplexed. "He'll think I'm a bit odd announcing that. I can do it now. I don't need help."

"Don't be so bloody stubborn woman. Go on."

I walk past the spectators towards the men's changing rooms and notice an extra body as I do. Harry. How long has he been there?

"Five minutes," I murmur as I pass. He's still as gorgeous as he ever was. I'd forgotten Mickey's long eyelashes were inherited from this man, and his cupid bow mouth and deep hazel eyes. It's like looking at Mickey all grown up. Terrifying.

"You ok?" asks John as I sit on a bench whilst he tidies up.

"I think so, " I blurt, " My son's Dad is sat outside."

He sits next to me, we both look at nothing but pegs full of coats.

"I didn't realise you were with him."

"I'm not. He wants Mickey. He's come to tell me he wants my son."

"I'm sorry." says John quietly.

"Hey, no need." I brighten, "how's about we all give him a good left hook? Right in the eye. That'll get rid of him, yeah?"

"It will. Then he'll be back, with the police, they'll close us down, and he'll have more ammunition to fight with." He smiles. "Besides, I don't think you'll be punching anyone with your fists for a couple of days."

"Why ever not, of course I will. I'll be back Friday, you wait and see."

"I've absolutely no doubt you will. You won't be sparring though. Give me your hands."

I place my gloved fists in his cupped hands. Turning my body to face him, I'm surprised at how gentle he is when he slowly rips the Velcro.

"Now here's the hard part, hold on." He warns, he looks deep into my eyes as he starts to pull my glove. Immediately soaring white hot burning pain shoots through my entire hand, up my arm. I begin to scream then hold it. Clenching my teeth instead.

The air hits my hand and a second wave of pain takes me. I feel dizzy, nauseous. I hold onto the bench to steady myself. John locks my knees between his own.

Without asking, he starts on my other hand. Quicker this time, my left. I think a chainsaw would be less painful. Giving birth twice would be. I can't bend my fingers, I daren't move my hands in case they catch something. Fabric, the bench, the wall anything. I don't want them to touch anything ever again.

John is shaking his head. I drop my head, still clenching my teeth, and John moves closer letting me rest on his chest as I get my breath. He strokes my hair, then stops suddenly.

"I'm so sorry, I shouldn't have let him. We do it with all boxers. It hardens their hands. Makes your knuckles scale like, calloused, rough. So you can handle more. It's against normal practice now, that's why I told him not to."

"It's my fault, always something to prove."

I look down to my hands and see the wet blood mixing with the dry. My little finger on both hands is purple and swollen until it looks like a mini sausage. Every knuckle of every finger is bloody. There's indents where tiny chunks of skin have been ripped away by the stitching on the new gloves. I feel a little relieved to know that it is this drying of blood that is stopping me bend my fingers and not broken bones, although my little ones may need further investigation. I'm exhausted and defeated, as well as knowing that for the next week at least I will not be able to punch anything.

"I can't go and see Harry like this John. I can't."

John disappears around a corner for a second then returns with a white first aid box.

"I'll clean you up, then we'll use bandages yeah? Say they're wraps. Tell him you have to keep them on to strengthen your wrists. He won't know. You can dig your nails into my leg if you want."

I look into his amused blue eyes.

"Why?"

"Because this antiseptic is going to sting twice as much as that sparring ever did!"

Wouldn't you know it, he's right again.

Chapter 20

My hands bandaged and moveable I walk out of the changing rooms as the boys start flooding in. I see Harry sat, clean shaven, floppy hair, sparkling eyes and feel foolish for arranging to meet here. My heart skips a beat as our eyes meet. I'm wet with perspiration, I have waterproof mascara on and that's it. My hair is falling out of the ponytail, and quite frankly I'm starting to smell a bit. I need a shower. Any confidence I had whilst sparring evaporates as I see Harry has the upper hand.

As I lead the way out of the gym, I nod to John who's leaning against the changing room doorframe. He looks worried. Probably tired, just as I am.

Harry starts talking as soon as we're outside. The sharp air on my bandaged hands makes me flinch but I'm grateful for it keeping me alert.

"So why boxing?" He asks. There's a patronising tone to his voice, which I'd forgotten.

"Why not? Dad died, I need to be the protector now. What's it matter?"

"It matters that you are a mum, that is quite willing to damage herself all for a cheap sadistic buzz."

I want to hit him. I really want to hit him. I won't. I will. No. No.

"Everything's bad when you put a cruel spin on it Harry. If you have the twisted evil mind to think that way. I, however, have not. If a burglar broke into our house I stand a 50% better chance of defending my family than I did this time last week. Besides, I don't have to explain myself to you."

"I think once this ball is rolling, you will find that all you will be doing for the next few months, is explaining yourself to me Tina. My solicitors anyway. Where is Mickey?"

I point to the MacDonald's across the highway. Faint visions of families grabbing a late bite to eat fill the windows.

"Mickey could be any toddler over there. He could be with a friend you have never met yet he trusts dearly. He could be eating a Happy Meal right in front of your eyes and you wouldn't recognise him. You wouldn't KNOW your own son." My voice becomes louder as we approach the crossing. " You wouldn't KNOW because you have NEVER MET your OWN SON!"

As usual when I mix emotion with anger I shake. I'm shaking now. I have tears in my eyes, my teeth are chattering, and I can't think straight. I have left myself open for his attack. I will the lights to change so I can cross to the car park, to my car. Then speed away and never face this again. Leave the country, take Mickey, just flee. His voice is calm, the voice of someone who is confident in their victory, who doesn't need to shout to win. Who has nothing to prove or defend.

"The past doesn't matter. What matters is now. I am secure, I have a loving home waiting for Mickey. He will want for nothing. That's all the courts will see. He'll have the best life with me. I've arranged for a DNA test, this week. It's against the law not to comply."

"He won't have everything," I cry, "He needs his mum."

"You can visit. In between times, he'll have my mother. My mum is very excited about all of this."

The lights change and I run to the car. I lock every door and forget the pain in my hands as I drive away. It's not until I'm safely parked outside the house that I let myself go. I sob. I sob for Dad, for Gran, for Mickey, for mum, for myself. I shout out for Dad but nothing happens. Nobody comes.

I walk into the house and straight past mum. Mickey is sleeping soundly in bed. I check him, kiss him all over, and then hold him close. I need to know he's here. He's real, he's with me. I fight the urge to pack a bag and walk downstairs to greet mum instead.

I can hardly manage words. If I talk I will cry again. If I say it out loud it will make it real.

I stare at the TV not noticing what's on. Mum's in her dressing gown in her usual place in Dad's chair.

"What's with the bandages?" She asks.

"I was a bit silly, didn't wear my wraps. Hurt my hands a little bit." Small fib. Not major.

"I don't know why you want to hurt yourself the way you do?" Mum's concern is nearly too much to bear. I feel the tears moments away again.

"Mum, there's a lot more ways than that to hurt someone. Just because you can't see the wounds, it doesn't mean they don't run deep."

"I know that love. You mean your Dad?" She asks kindly.

"No, Harry." As soon as it's out, I feel selfish. Lighter, but selfish. This is my problem, there is no need to add to mum's grief. I'm only telling her so she can help me feel better.

"What about him. He rang so I'm guessing he wants to be part of Mickey's life. It would be good. Would do you good. You could do with a break every now and again

"He doesn't want to be part of his life mum." I start sobbing.

Mum rushes over to comfort me, putting an arm around my shoulder.

"Why?" She asks.

"He wants to be all of it. He wants to take Mickey away. For good. Forever."

Mums on her feet in a flash, battle pose perfected, she blusters.

"Over my dead body! He is NOT having Mickey. He is not. Why if I'd have known what he was up to when he rang the other night. I'd have given him a piece of my mind. No, I would have told him you'd left and I'd no idea where you'd gone. That would do it. In fact pack a bag, go now. Go, go to your grannies, your friends, down south, anywhere. I can find you somewhere until you settle, go."

Seeing mum's irrational behaviour gives me a problem I want to fix. I can see a solution, but it's not this. This isn't the way.

"I'm not leaving mum. I'm not leaving you, I'm not leaving our life. He'll only find us again. I've been talking to Gran and she thinks he has not one leg to stand on. The more I think, the more I see the sense."

"Sorry," mum sits back down. "Gut reaction".

"I wish Dad were here." I sigh.

"Yep, he'd sort it. With a couple of words or a punch on the nose. Harry wouldn't dare threaten this if your Dad was here, that's the whole point. I'm not your Dad Tinsey, but I'm still your mum, and I will try to be everything you're missing right now. I promise. Why didn't you tell me about this?"

"I didn't want to worry you mum."

"Seeing you worried worries me more. Not knowing worries me. I'm not made of glass, I can handle it. I'm here to help. What did your granny say about it all?"

I tell mum everything, beginning to end.

"You need a solicitor, that's the first thing. You can't fight solicitors. You need one, we can "what if?" all day, but as soon as you have a solicitor, you are armed. You're prepared at least. Trust me. We'll fix this."

Mum has a sparkle in her eye that's been missing of late, my guilt disappears. Maybe this will help another focus. Something else, somebody she can save.

Her words make sense and I'm reminded that although Dad has gone I'm not alone. I'm still lucky, and however tempting it may be I must not take for granted the people he left behind.

"Ok." I mutter. I feel better.

"Proactive not Reactive, that's what we need to be. We'll do it. He needs to know that we're still a force to be reckoned with!"

I smile as I take myself off to shower. My painkillers for migraines are helping with my hands. I wash my hair with my bandages still on. Yet when I've finished I sit on the closed loo seat and gingerly remove them.

Being wet, they come off quite easily, but nature makes me keep my hands in a claw shape. My fingers hooked. Putting on my nightclothes I flinch, then leave both hands on top of the duvet as I snuggle next to Mickey in my double bed.

I'm exhausted, both physically and mentally. A deep dreamless sleep would be welcome, however it seems someone else has other ideas. I find myself lying on the lawn of the garden. Dad's garden. The spiritual garden.

It's daylight. Dad is lying on his back looking at the sky.

"There's a train, look." He reaches his arm into the air, pointing to a cloud.

He looks in his early thirties. No bald patch. Amazing. His voice has not changed.

I clench my fists not wanting Dad to see me hurt, yet as I do I realise there's no pain. My hands are fine. Beautiful. No scars, no blood. I relax.

"Will we always have this Dad?" I ask, looking for the train.

"Have what Cherub?" He doesn't look at me.

"These dreams, these meetings. These lessons. Whatever they are."

"No."

No elaboration. That's it. End of discussion. Not likely.

"What do you mean, no?"

Dad sighs. As if he'd like to tell me everything but he can't.

"I'm hanging around, waiting for someone. Someone else will pass over soon; we will do our transition together. It will help them, to have someone here. Even though we all meet at the other side, I'm, well fortunate enough to have pegged it close to the time of this other person, so we'll do it together. It doesn't normally work like this. I'd be long gone, and next you'd hear from me would be when you died yourself."

"Who's dying? Mum, Granddad, Grandma?"

"Blimey, you really think I'd want to cross over with your granny? She hates my guts!"

I'm in shock. Gran said she was the next to go. If it's not her, then it could be anyone.

"Not grandma then."

"I can't tell you. I really can't. I've said enough. Anyway, well done. Taking my advice!"

"About what Dad?"

" The dog...you took my advice with the dog, and applied it to Harry."

"The dog was about Harry? You knew Harry would get back in touch? You knew what he was planning? How could you possibly know? Do you inherit fortune telling abilities when you die?"

I don't know if I'm angry or sad. If I feel protected or neglected. I had no idea the dog was about Harry. How could I? He hadn't even rung at that point.

"No, you silly sod," he laughs. "Being dead has its advantages. We don't predict the future, but we do get an overview. We can see everything happening at once. I could see Harry's conversations with his mother, their plans; I knew it was only a matter of time. His mother is such a bitter woman. Nothing good would come of him listening to her."

I get it.

"So now? Now what do I do. Carry on missing you until another dies, and you both disappear? Don't you miss us?"

Dad is as offended as a ghost can be.

"Of course I do. Everyday life, sharing things with you, nothing can compare to being alive with my family, but I can see the bigger picture here. Everything has a purpose. These problems are so little; because once I cross over, it will seem like only seconds until all of you are joining me. We will be together again, that's the main thing. Knowing that is all I need. You should believe."

"If I don't believe, what happens then? Am I struck down with lightening? Condemned to hell?"

"No," laughs Dad, "you'll just look a bit stupid when you get here, and you realise I was right all along."

This makes me laugh too. A low tickle in my belly at first. A little rumble. Then a huge vibrating belly laugh that explodes from my mouth like a stampede of horses. So loud, it wakes me. It's daylight, I'm rested, and once again my dead Dad has put a smile on my face.

Chapter 21

Five days later, I'm sat in a solicitor's waiting room. I'm overdressed in a suit I'd save for my bank manager, the idea of anything legal alien to me.

The Venetian blind and the free coffee make me nervous. Such a sterile environment, everything exacted to make the client feel nothing, surely it's just taking the sting out of the tail?

The receptionist smiles sympathetically whilst shuffling papers like a newsreader on her desk.

I'm tapping my foot. I'm impatient.

This morning I was ordered, by law to do something I don't want to. This doesn't sit very well. I'm a law abiding citizen, I follow the rules, file my tax returns, don't park on double yellow lines, so to be dragged to court for doing nothing, well, it leaves a bitter taste in my mouth.

A large smiley blond woman opens an office door to my right and stands back for me to enter.

"Mrs James, so nice to meet you. I'm Heather." I put down my coffee to shake her hand, she continues, "bring your coffee, do come in." She's so jolly, I wonder what she has in her own cup.

She closes the door behind me then takes a seat at the head of a table that would seat ten. She indicates for me to sit two spaces away to her left.

"I'm not Mrs James, that's my mother." I say as I remove my coat and hang it on the back of the chair.

"Oh, I am sorry. I thought this case involved a child?" No patronising voice, just genuine confusion.

"Yes it does. My son Mickey, however I didn't marry his father. Mickey was, well, a fortunate accident. His father didn't stay long enough to leave his name on the birth certificate." I relax, most of my talking done.

"Gosh. How judgemental must you think I am? When I heard custody battle, I assumed it was through a divorce. Well we all know what assume does don't we?"

"Makes an ass out of you and me?" I feel quite clever knowing this.

"Indeed. Well I hope I've got all the right paperwork, let's start again. Let's have the full story."

I start from the beginning, how Harry and I met. How I let him go, as I didn't want to hold him back, but how he made his choice to never see Mickey. I tell her about the absence. I tell her about his return, his threats and his patronising nature. I tell her that he's now very rich. Finally, I lay the letter I received this morning, on the huge table and push it towards her.

"Whoa!" Is all she can say as she opens it. She then reads through the rest quietly. She's most probably translating the gobbledegook that screamed madness at me when I tried to read past line five.

My hands begin to sweat a little.

"Right, without sounding like a cliché, there's good and bad news here. Before I go on, I need to know your ideal scenario. How would you like this to end? What do you see in the future for you, Mickey and Harry?"

"I don't see Harry in our future." Deadpan. Simple. Our life has been so simple. Not with all this complicated messiness.

"I won't lie to you Tina, that's really not an option. I know this is a very emotional time, but from a professional point of view, we need to be aiming for something a little more achievable. This man will be in your lives for eternity, as much as you despise the man, you do have to find some happy medium, if not for yourself, then for your child."

She is absolutely right. I'm being immature. I was wrong to think I could waltz off into the sunset, never having to share my boy. A boy needs his father, however much of a donut he is.

"It's not Harry I despise. A few days away from his mother and he's wonderful. However, she feeds him poison, he believes it. Alas, here we are."

"Well, I cannot fight this court order. If I'd have known about the application, I could have, at the time. Who was your solicitor then?"

I'm dumbfounded. Is it not obvious that this is my first time? I'm a lawyer virgin.

"I didn't have one."

"You must have received letters?"

"I think I did. However, I've had a little personal debt of late, I'm ashamed to say I ignored anything too official. I put them in a drawer. Not for long, just until I was in a position to pay. Which I am now. Dad dying kind of threw everything else out of the window. Insignificant compared."

"We can't change that now, we must work with what we have. You have to take Mickey in the morning for the DNA test. Shouldn't hurt. Unless, unless he's not the father?" She seems cheerful at this idea.

"No, he is. There's absolutely no doubt about that, and he knows it."

"Ok, so access. What access would you give?"

"I'd prefer none."

"I know. Realistically, if the DNA test proves he is the father, he will take the next step and try for custody. Now he can't do that until he's met Mickey. The courts like to try agreeable tactics first. Social services will become involved."

"Now that's just silly." This is scarier than Harry. All I've ever heard of social services is bad things. They take children away, put them somewhere worse. They ignore abuse in the children's homes.

"Not to take Mickey away. No, they have a department that after a few supervised visits, a member of this team will interview Mickey, find out what he wants. They do it with pictures.

He won't even know he's been asked questions. Then they will decide where Mickey is best off."

"What if they decide Mickey is best off living with his father? I'm not exactly rolling in it."

"It's not about the money. It's about the child's emotional and physical wellbeing. Ignore Harry's threats; he has very little chance of that happening. The most likely scenario is they'll suggest Harry takes Mickey for regular weekends. At the most shared care. Weekends, one night during the week and half the school holidays."

"He's not at school yet."

"You get the gist. It may not come to that. One step at a time. You will not lose your son. The DNA test results though will give him rights."

"What type of rights?"

"Well he'll have parental responsibility. This means he'll have a say in which school he goes to. You won't be able to leave the country with Mickey for longer than twenty nine days without his permission. His name, changing it by deed pole will be impossible without his consent. There's quite a lot. I have a leaflet, I'll leave you to read it."

It's a lot to take in. Bringing up Mickey alone I'd become quite possessive of the decision making.

"The most important factor you may want to consider though," she continues," is the making of a will. Without a will, if anything happens to you, Harry automatically gains custody of Mickey. No questions asked. Your family could fight it, but it would take a lot of time and money. Maybe money they won't have. With a will, your wishes are binding. Have your mum as proposed legal guardian, anyone. Then Harry will have to fight."

This fills me with dread. Never before have I been more scared of death than this moment. Not of the process, I've seen the afterlife, but of those, I'll leave behind, and how.

I feel physically sick, I have to go, I have to excuse myself. I start to retch "Toilet?" I mumble.

Heather stands and points in the direction of the bathroom.

I throw up the coffee. My stomach has turned, as if I've been instantly hit with food poisoning. I have a cold sweat and am in no doubt that if I looked in a mirror I would be as white as Joan of Arcs wedding dress.

I contemplate bypassing Heather's office to go straight home, but remember I left my bag. I'm not as strong as I thought I was.

She's shocked to see the change in me.

"Look that's enough for today. Just sign on here please, to say I am instructed to act on your behalf. I will write to Harry's solicitors and we'll see if we can't make this as smooth as possible. In the meantime, my secretary will make you an appointment with me for two weeks time. We should have the DNA results by then."

I raise my eyebrows, not trusting myself to speak.

"I've read through the letter, and Harry doesn't want any room for error. He has requested a blood test. Mickey has to have a small amount of blood taken. I'm sorry. It won't hurt; they are very good with children."

I shake my head and leave, before my brain explodes.

The next morning I reluctantly take the letter and Mickey to the hospital. Our appointment has been made for us, and although we could ring, make an excuse, suggest another day, it will only delay the inevitable. I decide to get it over and done with.

In the hospital waiting room I sit Mickey on my knee and try to explain.

"They will want to take a tiny bit of your blood Mickey." I smile softly.

"Why?" His big eyes look at me, trusting me completely.

"They want to test it. Just to see what type of blood it is."

"Tell them mummy, it's people blood. Not alien blood."

I laugh a sad laugh as his name's called out, and we're soon shown to a small side room with a bed, a chair and some strange machines. There's one doctor and two nurses.

They all introduce themselves, the male doctor talking like a baby to Mickey as he coats the back of his hand with an anaesthetic cream.

I keep tight hold of Mickey's other hand.

"Now then Mickey," he says,"The cream should be working now." He presses his nail into Mickey's hand. "Can you feel that Mickey."

Mickey shakes his head for no.

A nurse prepares a needle out of Mickey's eye line.

"Now Mickey, look at mummy," coos the doctor.

I try to wink, but instead just smile and stroke his cheek. I cannot help but watch as the needle goes in. It's clear Mickey feels every plunge as his body buckles on the bed.

His eyes wide he shouts straight at the doctor,

"That's my blood. Give me my blood back. That's MY blood."

I cry. As if I haven't done enough of that lately.

"Leave it, just leave it." I raise my voice.

A nurse grips my shoulders from behind and pulls me from the room, as another holds Mickey down so the doctor can fill the vial with Mickey's blood.

Mickey is still screaming.

"My grandaddy will punch you for hurting me. My grandaddy will kick your butt."

When the doctor is finished, I run to Mickey and scoop him up.

"I'm sorry, I'm sorry."

He says nothing. He wipes his snotty nose on my shoulder and is quiet. The calm after the storm.

I know what he's thinking though. "You lied to me."

How can I tell him that a stranger who's his daddy made me do it?

Chapter 22

Last night I got drunk. I got so drunk I was sick. It started quite innocently; I knew I needed something to help me sleep. The expectation of the DNA results on the doormat too much to bear.

For the past two weeks I have been fine. If it weren't for the grieving of Dad I'd say wonderful. I've known that Harry cannot do anything without those results. So for those two weeks we've been safe. Just like before. I've lost ten pounds in fat, gained four pounds in muscle; I'm only a few weeks away from the fight. I've been focused and happy, then it hit.

So I drank. I gave up the gauntlet and joined mum for an evening. It felt great, for an hour, until the room span, until I threw up. I did sleep well though. With hindsight, I could have done without it. The letter from the hospital is open in my hand, and I know Harry will have received something identical. No longer, can I run and hide, I have to stay and fight.

If only my eyes would stop closing, my stomach stop turning, my skin stop itching, if only I hadn't drank my shares in Smirnoff, I may be able to. I don't have time to go back to bed as the phone rings. Mickey is shopping with mum. The benefits of sharing a house with a live in babysitter highlighted today.

It's Heather on the phone.

"Tina, is that you?" She asks.

"Uh huh. No offence Heather, but please speak slowly and don't shout. I'm coming to see you this afternoon. Are you cancelling?"

"No, not at all. Have you got the results?"

"I have, I've just opened them. Heaven knows why I'm surprised, but yes, he's Mickey's dad."

"Ah. Yes, well. Their postman must be up with the lark, as I was welcomed to the office by a fax from Harry's solicitors. They have the results. Harry has claimed parental responsibility. He also rejects your offer of one weekend a month. He wants full custody"

"I thought he couldn't get full?" I gasp. My head is a little too fuzzy for this.

"Sorry," I hear papers rustling, Heather is always apologising, "I may not have explained it properly. Harry undoubtedly knows he won't get full custody, unless he's delusional of course, but he has to apply for the highest, he has to start from the top."

"Then he hopes he won't have too far to fall."

"Exactly. You may not like this, but think of haggling in the shop. That's exactly what you're doing now."

"There is no better bluffer than me, bar Dad."

"Well then, you've just found a way to play the game. So next instructions please bluffer."

"He can have one weekend a month and every second Sunday afternoon. After three months of supervised access. He is a stranger to Mickey, after all."

"Perfect. Right I'll fax that back and hopefully have another deal by the time I see you this afternoon. "

With a nap and a shower, I'm certain my afternoon comes quicker than Heather's. Mum on returning has offered to have Mickey until after I finish at boxing tonight. It's a relief. I still have the hangover complete with headache, although I'm finding it easier to speak than when I first woke up.

As I arrive at the office, Heather is bent over her receptionists desk, showing her some papers. She smiles brightly, and immediately stops the task in hand to give me her full attention. Without a word, I follow her to the same room. Today she indicates the chair just one place away from her.

"I've good news and bad news," she says, smiling.

I finish taking my coat off, then put my palms flat on the table to receive the news.

She doesn't wait for affirmation, she's so overjoyed, the words tumble out.

"He's agreed not to fight for full custody." She's almost bouncing up and down on her chair.

"What's the bad news then? There can't be any surely? That's the best news in the world, ever."

"No," Heather adopts a serious face, although I still see the grin. "He says he will do the supervised visits, but on an ad hoc basis. He personally believes Mickey will trust in him a lot sooner than three months."

"Ok. That's ok. So who supervises?"

"He's requested you do it."

"Me? Why on earth would he want me?"

"I don't know, but you can ask him yourself. First visit is Sunday afternoon, at your place."

"That's the day after tomorrow."

"Yep." Then the shuffling of papers again, giving me time to digest the information.

"Can we change the venue, just, well, it's not a very happy place our house at the moment. It's loving, just a little sad with Dad going, a park would be better. A park with a cafe in case it rains."

"I don't see it being a problem. I'll sort it out. Glen Gardens OK?"

I nod as she rises. The meeting is over.

"I'll ring you if there's a problem. The details are all here."

She hands me a rather bulky folder. "We'll still need the odd meeting. Of course, after the supervised visits you need to agree where to go next. Your will too, I'll sort out your will for you."

I thank her, and leave, happy that I seem to have her on my side. When night falls, I'm walking with heavy legs up the hill towards the boxing club. Never before have I entered feeling as bad as this. I almost talked myself out of it twice, yet I would just be letting myself down if I stayed home tonight. I have only two weeks until the fight. I've been here every open evening. I've developed a relationship with my trainers, a new respect; I couldn't throw it all away on a hangover. Plenty of people do workouts with hangovers, why should I be any different.

I peer through the half open door, and my heart skips a beat at what I see. John is training our newest and youngest recruit. A mere ten years old, he's teaching him how to skip. I want to take a picture, but soppiness is not welcome here.

"Whatcha standing there for?" shouts Lenny. "Get your arse in here."

The men of the club didn't swear for the first fortnight, even the trainers. What a lovely mannered bunch of men I thought they were. That was until I dropped my first f word whilst sparring, and now every second word is an expletive from their mouths. More relaxed for it they are too. Golly gosh doesn't sound apt after being given a black eye. No matter whom you are.

Dad was a big curser. I blame it on his pure London roots. It didn't sound strange though. He never offended with his swearing, no matter how posh the person. Odd how I'd not heard him swear much now he's dead. I'll have to ask about that.

There are already two fully grown men sparring in the ring. They have the protective headgear on as well as the crotch gear. John got hold of some breast plates for me last week, so I too look a little odd when sparring. This only crosses my mind for a second though, it's all my mind has time for once I start.

The fight is good. Tommy is being referee. A place he fits in well. He sees me at the side, and as he winks, one of the sparer's gives a full blow to the other. The bell is forced as blood hits the canvas. Fight over.. It's been a while since anyone fought, some of the boys are itching to release their wrath, yet sparring teaches control. How to pull back, how to defend. It's not for injuries or pummelling each other. It doesn't stop some trying though. Callum's mum smiles from the spectator's chairs, so I sit next to her. The ring is only six feet away. I would love, right now to curl up and watch the sparring, learn a few things. That would be a lovely evening for me. Gentle, yet productive. The purposeful way Lenny is striding towards me, makes it seem only that. A dream. Without speaking, he takes my bare hands quite roughly, then tips my backpack upside down. He grabs one of my wraps whilst still gripping tightly to my hands.

I look to Vicky, she shrugs.

"Evening to you too Lenny, " I say, trying my hand at humour to lighten the situation. John looks over the head of the boy he's training, he moves his head, subconsciously trying to hear the exchange between Lenny and I. It's not easy, over the bell, the barked instructions, the grunts, the whack of the skipping ropes.

That's it! I'm late. I must be at least half an hour late. No one is running. It's over, I've missed the run. Phew. That feels good.

I wince a little as Lenny pulls tightly on the second wrap.

"I need these wraps on tightly. Your hands heal quick, that's good. However what I have planned for you tonight has been known to break wrists without wraps on." He seems happy at this thought.

"Not tonight, eh Lenny, I'm feeling a little fragile tonight."

He stands, towering over me, "you think I don't fucking know that? I see you walking in here less energy than a fucking tortoise. Five months we've been at this, you should know by now, your bed, it's for sleeping in, you hear me?"

Lenny is not referring to sex here, oh no. The trainers actually encourage it for exercise. He's referring to me reading until the early hours, as strange as it seems I share my love of books with all the trainers. Mostly John, but owning a bookshop I can chat about Lenny's westerns as if I've read them all.

"It's not that Lenny; it's not, a little hangover that's all."

He shakes his head, "you need to make a choice, Tina."

He finishes off, then shouts four inches from my face, "RUN".

And I do. I've become used to following the orders, I actually like relinquishing control for a little bit. I feel free. My mind soars. Tonight though my aching body and nauseous stomach bring it back to earth. This feels like torture.

I do ten laps of the gym, all the time Lenny shouting orders, left hand down, right hand down, drop and give him ten. I slow to a fast walk when I see him holding a skipping rope at the other end of the gym. I don't break step as I take it off him and stand a few feet away from John and the new boy.

My feet have become light over the last few weeks, yet today, once again I feel as if I am lifting a baby elephant with every jump. My head pounds, but I keep on. Stopping is not an option. I know once the skipping's over, there won't be long left. I shouldn't be thinking like this, I'd never clock watched before. Painkillers, hot bath, horlicks and bed, how boring had my life become when I became almost alert at the thought of this combination.

Tommy looks over from the ringside, he has smaller boys in there now, they're just finishing off.

"You brought your mouth guard?" He shouts.

I start to lie, but Vicky beats me to it.

"Yes she has." She wipes off the dust with her jumper as she picks it up from the floor. It must have shaken out when Lenny got my wraps.

I'm still skipping, he takes pity.

"Go on, on the bag, I'll be there in a minute. That's the last time you will decline a spar, do you hear me?"

I nod, and stop next to Vicky for a drink of water.

Lenny uses a rough towel to rub me down. It's a guaranteed way to lose the weight. Of course, once training stops it piles back on again. Sixty percent of what we lose is water, yet boxing is not about health really. It's not good for a body the extremes that boxing takes it to. No wonder the careers are so short.

"This sweat," he tuts, "is pure flipping vodka!"

He walks away feigning disgust, so a male spectator holds the bag steady for me.

"Combinations!" Shouts Tommy from the ringside.

So I do. I can feel how weak my punches are. The helper is hardly moving. My arms ache, I am disappointed with myself, and no matter how hard I try to make the next combination work, it doesn't.

I manage ten rounds then stop. Tommy gestures me over. I sit on the side of the ring, and he talks to me from inside the ropes.

"See him there," he points to a six foot man sparring. He's huge, and powerful.

"You're better than him in a lot of ways. Granted your footwork needs honing, but you're two punches ahead. Your left jab is fast, and your reflexes lightening. He's stronger, but lazy."

I've heard it before, normally I'm proud, and tonight I shake my head as if he has the wrong girl.

"GET UP!" He screams. " Now take the fucking feather duster out of your hand and fucking hit it!" he's holding the bag.

I hit it.

"HARDER!" He shouts. "One, Two. One two, three. One, Two. Two, One. One two Three, Four. Six, combo, six, now five, go on, faster, do it!"

I do, a last gasp. Nearly falling over. The bell goes.

Tommy is smiling. "Now don't EVER tell me you can't do it again! Go home, rest. See you Monday!"

I want to kill him and kiss him all at the same time. I leave feeling ashamed of myself.

Mum and Mickey are already in bed by the time I get home. I think I must have taken the long route, my mind doesn't remember the journey. I poke the last embers on the fire then curl up on dad's chair. I dial Gran's number, needing acceptance, just somebody to tell me they think I'm wonderful no matter what. Gran is my ego booster.

It rings and she answers. I say hello then burst into tears. I don't stop for a full hour.

Chapter 23

"Who is he?" Asks Mickey. The question I have been dreading. What do you tell a three year old? I kneel down to position his hat properly and kiss him on the nose.

"He is a friend of mummy's darling, but he'd like to be a friend of yours too."

That's not lying. I don't agree with blurting out that it's his long lost father. Harry could well disappear again, leaving one distraught little boy. This is safer. This will protect him.

"Will he buy me an ice cream?" He asks, satisfied with my answer.

"It's a little cold for ice cream darling, but let's see shall we? Come on."

Yes, you've guessed it, it's already Sunday. Sunday afternoon in fact and mother and son are going for an innocent stroll around the park, maybe meeting a friend for afternoon tea, how quaint.

Do you ever play the people game? Do you ever look people and guess who they are, where they're going? I do.

I don't think in my strangest depths of imagination, however, that I would look today and say, "yes she's obviously a single mother grieving for her dead father, has paranormal tendencies and boxes in her spare time. Whilst he is meeting the son he fathered over four years ago but has only today gained the courage to actually meet."

This park is wonderful. There are cute little tables on a lawned garden, whilst at the end are swings, climbing frames, seesaws and slides. To the right is a huge pond with pedal boats and just behind us is crazy golf and trampolines. If you stretch your eyes a little over the tables, you'll see a cliff edge and a deep blue sea on the horizon.

It's a popular venue for concerts, yet during the day; it has an upmarket family feel.

Harry is already sat at a table. He has a cafeteria of coffee, two cups, and a can of coca cola waiting. I instinctively grip Mickey's hand tighter.

He looks up at me then follows my gaze to Harry. I have to stop, I have to take everything in, I don't feel comfortable taking the next few steps. My heart is pounding in my throat, I feel nauseous, I could pass out.

I do.

I come round only moments later wrapped in a cashmere arm, my bum on a cast iron chair. Mickey is sat drinking a glass of milk opposite me, he's chattering away to Harry as if he's known him all his life. My immediate reaction is to push the arm away. I still feel a little dizzy, but compose myself and with a shaking hand help myself to cream.

"Well I never thought you'd fall for me a second time, but now you have it's made my day!" Laughs Harry. He winks at Mickey; they have a private joke, already.

"Sorry, sorry, I don't know what came over me. I don't. I'm back now, anyhow, Harry this is."

"Mickey. Yes we've met. I asked the waitress for milk as Mickey tells me Coca cola has too many Bees in it?"

Mickey smiles broadly. I shuffle over to be closer to him, I want to swallow him up in my arms, I'm so proud.

"So, " Harry continues, "Mickey was asking who I am."

Oh dear. The outcome of this all depends on whether Harry has had a little pep talk from his mother when he left the house. He does seem a little different today though. More relaxed, happier, almost flirting.

"Yes, I told Mickey we were friends." I said, trying to give Harry some signal with my eyes.

"I thought as much. I'd like to be Mickey's friend too though, if that's ok with mummy of course?"

Now where was Harry hiding?

"Twampoline, twampoline!" shouts Mickey, before I've a chance to answer. Bless three year old children and their short attention spans. I crane my neck to look at them.

"You finish your coffee, " says Harry, "and I'll walk him over. You need the sugar I think, you've been training too hard."

I finish my coffee in an undignified gulp.

"No, no," I fish a ten pound note from my faux Chanel bag, " I'm here, I'm coming."

This new Harry has unnerved me, what's to say his evil mother isn't lying in wait in a box hedge somewhere, just waiting for the opportunity to grab Mickey and brainwash him with a loads of codswallop?

I'm not taking any chances. Oh I'd love to spar with that woman. As I almost jog to keep up with them, I ask Harry, "So how's your mother? I half expected her to be here today?" I try to make it sound innocent, although I couldn't disguise the smattering of venom on every word.

"Let's get Mickey on the trampoline, and we'll have a chat eh?" He winks again.

He either has a twitch or has recently bought, "How to Win Friends and Influence People using sign language."

I let him sort Mickey out; I take pleasure in watching him struggle. I have no plans to make this easy for him; as far as I can see I have done most of the hard work. The sleepless nights, the potty training, (not there yet), the full works, and he is waltzing in just as Mickey is capable of conversation, a fact which makes parenting a hundred percent easier.

I wouldn't change those early years for the world, although I would like to throw a few dirty nappies in Harry's face right now.

He copes rather well for an amateur. He may have nieces and nephews, I've not asked.

I fold my arms and cross my legs on the bench. Mickey is shouting loudly jumping up and down in the caged trampoline. Harry has paid for five minutes.

He sits next to me, as he shuffles along with his hands in his suede coat pockets, I try to shuffle away. The wooden bench is only so long before I'm squashed in the corner.

"I'm not going to jump on you, you know!" He says, laughing.

"To be fair, Harry, I never can tell. Last time we met you weren't exactly pleasant."

"No, I wasn't." He looks off into the distance. Towards the sea. "I was jealous. Jealous, angry and bitter. I'm sorry. My mother wound me up to such a degree, and then seeing you there, in that boxing club, looking, so well, fit! I just couldn't handle that you weren't mine. I couldn't. My reaction was wrong, but I wanted to be on your mind, I wanted to be the only thing on your mind. Bar Mickey of course."

"Well you certainly achieved that Harry. I have been worried sick. You and your mother were trying to gain full custody of Mickey. I hope you never have to understand just what pain that causes for a mother. I wouldn't wish it on my worst enemy Harry, yet you did. You did it to me."

He tries to take one of my hands, to uncross my arms, I don't want that I stay put. He has a tear in his eye as Mickey shouts to us. "More more!"

We nod in unison and the trampoline attendant sets the timer again.

"I'm so sorry Tina. I thought leaving you and Mickey was the best thing I could do, for everyone. For me. For a while it was. I had no ties, I could go wherever, see whoever I wanted. Being part of the band I had a great lifestyle, except when the parties over and everyone goes home, there's no one left. Lee has a baby now, did you know? He's settled down. As much as he ever will."

Any other time I would have gossiped away about this, I thought Lee was such a great person, but such a bad influence. This was real news. The timer has four and a half minutes left, we don't have time for gossip.

"That's all well and good Harry. I feel for you, I do. Except whilst you were partying, deciding what you wanted for the future, we got on with our lives, we moved on."

"I know, and you did a marvellous job raising our son. You have, my mother wouldn't even be able to deny that."

"Ok, what about your mother. You can't deny she's poison Harry. Encouraging you to fight the way you have. I can't forget how you listened. I would have thought you had a little more respect for me than that." I understand every word, I don't forgive though.

"You don't understand do you Tina? You just don't get it. Look at me."

I reluctantly turn to look him in the eye. His sparkling blue irises are so soft, glistening with the tears, I feel like crying with him, though I don't know why.

He's successful at pulling my arms apart, our knees touch as he holds my hands in his, rubbing them all the time to stave off the bitter chill.

"What?" I ask. I'm quite embarrassed. I've not had a man hold my hand in a un-boxing related way for years.

"I didn't see it as fighting for Mickey, sweetheart. I saw it as fighting for you! For you both, for my family. That's what you are, both of you. Whether you like it or not. I want you back Tina."

Times up!

As the attendant helps Mickey with his shoes, I ask a few quick questions.

"Your mother, what about your mother?"

"I humour my mother, you should know that. I can't change her, nobody will ever be good enough for her son, but I can make her accept it."

"But my Dad, my Dad said you were hatching a plan. You were discussing together how to take Mickey from me. How to gain custody. Why would he lie?"
As soon as I've said this, I realise my error. For the first time I have crossed my paranormal visions with life on earth. I attempt a giggle.

"How could he have possibly said that? I didn't think of custody until I read your Dad's memorial in the paper, so unless you're talking to the dead now?"
"No, no, no, no. No, I meant Grandad. My granddad often sees your mum, shopping about the town. That's what it is. She must have mentioned Mickey, and he warned me that's all."

He believes me. I wouldn't, but then I know the truth. I suppose to anyone it's easier to believe the simplest explanation.

"I was, I won't deny, talking to mum about custody of Mickey. Like I said though, I thought I was fighting for you too."
"But you didn't say that to your mum?"

"Gosh no. No, best to humour her. She'll grow to love you over time, just like I did."

"Where is she now?"

Mickey is by now holding onto my leg, I scoop him up and start walking towards the swings. I don't worry about him hearing this last question, it is all innocent.

After a two-minute silence, we reach our destination. I sit on an adult swing next to Mickey's toddler one, whilst Harry pushes Mickey gently backwards and forwards.

"If you must know, she's at my house, doing my ironing for me."

"I don't know why you feel the need to hide it Harry. Seriously, I don't think I'll ever be able to let my baby boy go. I empathise with her, I really do."

"So you understand why I can't say to her what I've just said to you? Not for a while, I don't want to upset her you see?"

I position my feet and push myself back and glide into the air. I shout down to the boys,

"Yes, but I'm in need of a lover, not an extra child!"

"I'll change, " he shouts up to me. Mickey laughs, he likes the game.

"Please just think about it. I'll be whatever you want me to be. "

I come to a stop and tickle Mickey on the head, laughing with him.

"And there lies the problem Harry."

Chapter 24

I can hardly move or talk. My brain is thinking double quick; if I breathe too slowly, I may just have a panic attack. I'm pacing around an unfamiliar changing room. It's seems odd as it's almost empty. I'm all in my kit and despite this place being free of plaster dust, my mouth is dry. I take a mouthful of water and then spit it out in the sink. I can't afford an extra ounce if I'm to be light on my feet; this mantra has been burned on my brain. Looking in the mirror, I don't recognise the person staring back. I have huge dark circles under my eyes; my skin is a deathly white. I can almost see my head throbbing. The pain kept at bay with the painkillers, yet the ache behind my eyes still evident. The adrenalin is the only thing keeping me upright. If a doctor saw me now, I'm sure he'd send me to bed not into the ring.

The irony is, if this were not just an amateur fight I would have a doctor. He would have checked me already. My family would also be close by, there is no one?

Mum is home looking after Mickey. By her own admission, she didn't want to come tonight. As a mother, I can completely understand if anyone hurt my Mickey I'd be jumping into the ring and ripping their limbs out, as a daughter, I would have liked her here. It's an achievement, coming this far, learning such a skill, it seems a shame not to share it with those you love.

Gran is also at home, her emphysema a little worse with the cold snap. In truth, I think she's staying away for the same reason as mum. I don't blame them.

I've made up my mind for this to be my one and only fight. I've trained so hard for it; my body has acclimatised to dehydration. I had something to prove, and regardless of the outcome, I think I've achieved my goal. Ideally, I'd like to walk away now, my yellow belly showing its true colour, yet I know I will be letting the whole boxing club down if I do. The boys, my second family are out there. All except one. John.

He said he couldn't bear to watch. So stuff him.

Lenny and Tommy are fussing around me as if I were the queen herself; I can see why boxer's egos grow quite large. If it weren't for the pounding my head would have grown in the last five minutes alone.

Tommy takes my hands and starts putting on my wraps.

"Now remember to snap that right jab yeah? Don't forget. Lock the shoulder too. We want nice clean lines. This is an amateur fight; you know there's little chance of anyone being knocked out? So aim for the points. Keep your footwork tidy, your combinations where you can."

"And keep you back foot on the fucking ground!" Laughs Lenny. It's a bad habit of mine.

"And your defences UP! Remember that first time? The first time you came into the club, with your pot belly and your wobbly arms?"

I nod, I don't trust myself to speak, we've developed such a bond over the last six months, I wish John were here too.

"She didn't make that mistake though, did she Tom?" Says Lenny.

"Nope. It's why we kept you on, do you know that? See most boys or men come to train because they want the kudos of being a boxer, you didn't. We saw that, and you know how? We have a little test you know? People who fail, never know we were testing them at all."

"Go on." I whisper.

"Well your first proper left hook, the one where you knocked Simon's sunglasses off his head, that one. Well ninety nine per cent of the boxers in that gym would have puffed out their chest and done a victory lap, they'd have been so proud of themselves. I've seen it so many times. It usually loses them the fight. Whilst they're soaking up the glory, the opponent is seeing a golden opportunity to knock them on their arse."

"That makes sense. So what did I do?" I'm physically shaking now, as if it's suddenly become cold. I know the fight is imminent. I put the shakes down to nerves. Tommy holds my hands tighter; is he's noticed he ignores it.

"You carried on. You must have known it was a knockout punch. The gym cheered. It didn't stop you though, you kept your defences up, your footwork light and ready, ready for his retaliation. Of course, it didn't come, but we knew then we wouldn't have to waste six months knocking out your ego, only to build it back up again."

Lenny is nodding quietly whilst folding towels onto the bench.

"We may not have had many heart to hearts you know Tina, "says Tommy, "but we do recognise a damaged person when we see one."

"I'm not damaged," I protest.

"There's something broken about you, you can't deny it. You wouldn't have embraced this sport so readily if there wasn't. "

"My Dad, he died, a week before I started."

"Who was he?" Asks Lenny, his ears perking up.

"Michael James, you won't know him, Dad grew up in the south."

"In Battersea?" Asks Lenny, and I realise why his accent was so familiar on my first visit. It's exactly the same as Dad's except a little more watered down.

"Yeah, how'd you know that?"

Tommy walks away to find my gloves. Lenny sits next to me on the bench.

"I trained him. Battersea Boys Club. Your dad was a pretty mean boxer. Featherweight at the time. I was sorry to lose him, but he moved up North when he got a job as a roady for the Beatles, and we heard nothing more. He'd been coming to the club since he was ten. Poor little sod he was then. I think I was the father he never really had."

Dad had often told me stories of his boxing days, his trainers, it was a big reason why I loved the sport in the first place, but I never put this equation together. It's reassuring.

"You've my mum to blame for him staying up here, he was quite smitten. Thank goodness. He stopped being a roady when he met her, opened shops, settled down – ish. You must have been only a few miles apart for years."

"Yeah. I saw a memorial in the paper, and he came to mind again, but there are so many

Michael James' I just assumed it couldn't be him."

"Well, it was. What a coincidence."

"Or twist of fate," pipes up Tommy. "I believe in fate. Something brought you here. It must have. We haven't time to think though; we have to get out there. You ready?"

"As I'll ever be."

I start jumping up and down on the spot. Not because I'd seen other fighters do it, but because my veins are tickling with the blood rush, it's the only thing to do to stop me from exploding. In a matter of minutes, this will all be over, and I will be home cuddled up with Mickey, telling mum how I'm giving it up, how I've done what I set out to do. The end.

Tommy pushes me forward so that he and Lenny can walk behind me. My kit is nothing special and I don't have a hooded gown. I'm wearing nylon shorts, black with a thin white line, and a black T-bar vest, which I've been told shows my new shoulder muscles off to perfection.

We have an unhindered walk to the ring. There's not a huge crowd of people to pass through. The lights to the sports hall are all on, so there's no spotlight. No build up, any fireworks, just a clap, from about thirty people. There's all of my training buddies, and Harry.

He's stood in the furthest corner near the entrance. Oh Harry step into the ring right now, I want to knock some sense into you dear boy!

This makes me a little more nervous, and gives me something akin to stage fright. The ring is a stage and I have the leading role. Strange when I think I took up boxing to escape attention. Tommy runs forward to part the ropes and I step through. I have the blue corner. I am the last to arrive, my opponent is already here.

She's all dressed in emerald green, even her gloves. I've never seen green gloves on the market, I'm impressed. I smile at her and she scowls. What did I expect? Tea and cake? She doesn't look too scary, not huge, not butch, just a normal fit girl about to punch my lights out. Here goes.

The referee is a skinny man, maybe they thought they needed no one bigger to come between two women? I wouldn't like to clip him round the ear, he'd probably snap. He indicates for us to meet and greet, and then the bell goes.

For a whole minute, we pussyfoot around. We throw punches that hit thin air, we shadow box feet away from each other, neither of us wanting to drop our defence to give that right hook, the risk too great to take for a first round.

I can just make out Harry in the corner of my eye, I shouldn't, I should be concentrating fully on this, and then WHAM.

She has me. My left eyebrow feels as if it's going to explode, yet instead of wanting to sit and cry, as I would had I banged it on a door at home, I want instant revenge.

I move closer to her, keeping my back foot down at all times, she blocks my first combination, but my on the second of my one two I hit her mouth. I'm not stopping, I go for her kidneys with my left hook but she grabs my neck in a clinch. The bell goes and the rounds over.

I crouch at the side of the ring. It was my request not to have a stool. I'd seen so much death lately; I was terrified of ending up like Hilary Swank in Million Dollar Baby.

Lenny mops my bloody brow. It makes me feel alive. It's certainly taken away my headache.

"If you weren't too busy checking on your boyfriend, you wouldn't have this cut." Scolds Tommy.

"He's not my boyfriend." I argue.

"Don't deny it," he smirks, " John saw you cuddling in the park a few weeks back, why'd you think he's left you be?"

Before I have a chance to put Tommy straight the bell sounds and I'm up. Plenty of time later. It does make sense though. John has been an absolute true friend, but I did think he would have asked for a date by now. The chemistry between us is electric, which in my experience is pretty rare. He must have felt it too. I make a mental note to put Tommy and Lenny straight as soon as the fight is over. John will then hear soon enough. They could be bigger gossipers than women, men, in the right setting.

I start playing in the next round, still absolutely pumped full of energy I ignore the pain and pretend I'm sparring in my own gym. The girl is very good, and it's almost a pleasure to have my abilities tested. When I land a great right jab on her cheek, I don't puff out my chest, but I do turn to the shuffling near Harry. My brain tells me I have half a second to register what's going on. I am pleased I have, as Gran has rode into the entrance in her scooter, she gives me the thumbs up, before falling off her seat in a heap, I turn my head just in time for my opponents revenge punch to hit me square on the temple, and I drop. I see the canvas rushing towards me but my arms won't move to stop my head hitting it. My whole body is numb. My brain braces itself for the impact, an impact that doesn't come, as I float. Everything disappears, like so many times before, and I find myself once again in dad's garden.

No, wait, the topiary is different, silly animals and balloons, there's even a hand giving the "up yours" sign. Dad is smiling, a huge smile, stood in the middle of the lawn. There's an opening in the hedge behind him, and now I can see the babbling brook I'd often heard. Crystals filled the pools glistening in a bright warm sunlight.

I feel nothing, no headache, no pain, nothing.

"What's happening Dad, why am I here? Am I unconscious?"

"No, cherub," says Dad. He seems so happy. "Remember I said I was waiting for someone, to help them cross over? That someone, Tinsey, is you."

Epilogue

"I can't go dad, I can't." Although I'm saying the words, I don't actually feel as worried or as sad as I thought I would. It's a strange feeling. Awake I would be crying at the prospect of leaving everyone behind, of Mickey growing up without his mum, but here, well. It's not that it doesn't matter. It does. It just doesn't matter enough.

That sounds bizarre, but it feels so right. I will see everyone very soon, and they too will feel this freedom. I am not so important that I should live whilst each minute others die.

I take Dads hand and we turn to face the arch.

"What about Mickey Dad?" I ask softly.

"Your mum will bring him up; he won't be short of love. He'll give her a reason to live again."

"I wanted to help him grow up. I wanted to be there. I was looking forward to every step."

"Me too Tinsey. Apparently, once we cross over we can watch now and again. We can even help a little, I don't know how, it's quite a mystery for me, and I've not been further than this garden, waiting for you."

"Did you know it was me you were waiting for?"

"Not entirely, no. I saw though, your headaches, your deterioration. I saw it all. It didn't take a genius. Plus you have that knack, you never lost it as a child, you can sense things, see people, dead people, me. Only children or people with one foot in the grave can do that. I hoped it wouldn't be you, but I'm happy it is."

I don't ask Dad to make any sense as I know exactly what he means.

"So mum? She won't cope. Why didn't you take mum? She would love to be here with you right now."

"I don't have a choice. I would love to have your mother, but she has a whole life ahead of her, whether she wants it or not. Mickey will open her eyes to it; she may even fall in love again, if she lets it happen."

"If she moves on?"

"Kind of, I'll be waiting, we'll be waiting."

"Let's go then." The pair of us walks towards the arch, the crystals shine brighter, almost blinding in the brook, there's a song, more warmth, we instinctively shield our eyes, although nobody can be harmed here.

"WAIT!" A familiar voice shouts loudly behind us. I stop, but Dad keeps going, I pull him back.

Grandma is running to us. Grandma is running. Without a mobility scooter, without a walking stick, her back is straight, and she is actually running. She's not out of breath. "STOP!" She shouts.

We do. I'm surprised to see Dad has only a smile on his face at greeting her, and not the scowl that was trademark of our family gatherings. Gran is also pleased to see him.

"Take me, Mike, take me."

"I don't think it's your turn Jean not for another year. You need to help Sylvie through this crisis, she needs her mum."

"So does Mickey, Mike please, just take me?"

I remember Dad telling me he would never transit with Grandma. Although I'd been caught up in it all, being able to hold Mickey and mum close to me fills me with absolute joy. I haven't been here long, but I know Grandma is pleading with the wrong person.

"Tinsey's time is up, Jean I can't change that."

"You were waiting for someone yes?" Oh ok, we do have telepathy here. Funny that, thought it was a myth. We understand everything now.

"Well," Gran continues, "take me. It won't upset any balance, I'll come quietly and just wait for everyone else to join us when they're old and ready."

"Then who goes when you're supposed to die?" Asks Dad.

"Doesn't matter. Let's just give this a go, give a baby boy his mummy back eh?"

Dad shrugs, not unkindly. He kisses me on the head as he releases my hand. He then takes Grandmas. I'm still expecting him to shudder at the mere thought, he doesn't.

They walk towards the hedge, towards the stream. Gran protects her eyes, but dad doesn't this time, and then it all goes black.

Black and cold. Absolutely freezing. With pain. My body is convulsing violently up and down, an extreme attack of shivers. I can't control it, and it hurts like the worst pain in my life. My head feels as if a saw has been taken to it, my lungs devoid of air. There is so much pain, and darkness. I try to move my arms and legs but they are stuck in some horrid kind of treacle. I feel my heart pound, my panic sets in, I buckle again, a stab into my right thigh and I relax.

It's still dark, it's still very cold, and the pain however, floats away. I hear a voice, a man's voice; I feel a tingling through the treacle in my fingers. Somebody has my hand. Is it Dad? Did he catch me when I fell? Where am I?

The voice again.

"Tinsey, Tinsey, open your eyes. That's all you have to do. Please open your eyes."

I try, they feel stuck together, like the sand from the deepest sleep. I try.

"Cold." I mutter. My own voice aloud makes me flinch.

Another voice, a ladies voice.

"We're trying to wake you up Tina. Open your eyes, we will make you warm."

Like the prying open of a two tonne metal portcullis using only a crowbar I do, a slit at first, then the light is back. The blinding light. It hurts, I close my eyes again.

I feel someone touching my face, putting glasses on me.

The lady's voice again, "I'm sorry, my fault, try again."

I open them again, and it's darker this time, a pink hazy light. Much better, I can see.

I hear mumbles, the lady puts some blankets over me then it's quiet. Nothing. I try to move but can't. I can feel a pipe in my nose, another in my arm, when I raise my head it's very dizzy and a bit slushy. As if there's water gushing around splashing on the sides of my skull.

My hand tingles again and then cramps, as if it's back in wraps. It takes me a moment to digest that it is touching skin, someone is holding it.

"Mickey? Mum?" I ask in my mono syllabic tongue.

"They're on their way. Your mums taking Mickey out of nursery." The voice, I recognise the voice. It's John. I try to squeeze my hand around his. I don't know if I've achieved my aim.

"John, I'm sorry, I lost."

"Don't be so silly. We thought you were a gonner. You've scared us all."

"Where am I?"

"Hospital. You've had an operation. You had tumours. They think they've got them all."

"In my head?"

"Yep. Fates see. They wouldn't have spotted them if they hadn't given you a skull X-ray after the fight. If your opponent had of knocked you down using a kidney blow, they would never have X-rayed your head."

"That's good then". I try to smile but something restricts my mouth. There's some kind of metal guard.

"Just relax for now, you've been sedated for over two weeks, your body can't take this much. Your guard will come off today. Another week or so, you can come home."

"I'm alive then?"

"Yes, you're alive. I'm going to keep you that way too. No fighting you hear?"

"Yep. Gran, where's Gran?" I think maybe it was all a dream.

"I'm sorry, she's gone."

I try to nod, but can't.

A week later, Mum, Mickey, Lenny, Tommy, and John arrive to pick me up take me home. I've enjoyed my rest. I've enjoyed the visitors. Every one of them more precious. There's a lot to be said for being free of worry and pain, but a lot to be said for touch, emotion, cuddles and laughter too. I'm not ready to give that up, not just yet.

"So Sylvie," says John, "you babysitting whilst I take your daughter out for dinner tonight?"

"She'd have a job," pipes up Tommy, "I've already asked if she'd celebrate by coming for a meal with me."

"Just leaves you Lenny, "I giggle.

"How's about we all stay in. I'll cook. We'll have a wilder party when Tina's out of the wheelchair!" Cheers mum.

Everyone nods. Mickey climbs on my knee and hugs me close to his face.

The vision in my left eye goes a little blurry and I see Dad and Grandma standing plain as day smiling and waving, giving the thumbs up. There's no garden, no special setting, just them.

The feeling suddenly hits me that my paranormal adventures have just begun.

See the end of the book for an extract from Martina Mercer's next novel, "The Sins of the Next Generation".

Acknowledgements

Does anyone actually read this page? Apart from the wonderful people I've promised to mention.

During the writing and endless proof reading, I have used this page as a bribe, a favour, payment even and I'm very proud to say that I must have absolutely wonderful friends, fans and family if the only payment they wanted was recognition for their efforts.

To my late father, Michael James. Without whom this story would never be told. Who taught me I could fulfil any dream I wanted to as long as I was prepared to work hard enough. Who gave me the morals I have today, who loved me unconditionally, who shattered my world when he died at the young age of fifty but left me the strength to carry on, somehow.

To mum. My original proof reader, who didn't balk when a few moments I'd taken from our personal lives were used for dramatic effect. For giving me the confidence to be who I am today, my best friend. Thank you. I love you.

My children, for being excited, for spurring me on, for knowing that even though I'm a workaholic, I am chasing a dream, our dream, for never letting me forget the reason I'm chasing it.

To colleagues, and subsequent friends. To Lindsay Riley, a great character for the next book, not one to mince her words, for giving me a kick up the bum when I would rather be watching the clouds with my loved ones.

Serena Van De Meulen Taylor for being the best friend I could ask for. For proof reading for free.

To my old drama and English teacher, Richard Grayson. Thank you for not letting mini me put you off working with me as an adult.

My brother, Lee James for being a distant fan, my aunty Sally Stephenson for being a closer one.

Fellow authors, including Freya North for their support and encouragement.

Wild Wolf Publishing for taking a risk.

Lastly, my husband Justin Mercer-Phillips for having half a me whilst I work, for putting up with the fact that I still work when the computer's turned off and the day is over, and for believing in me and for being the most genuine man I have ever met since Dad. Thank you.

The Sins of the Next Generation (available summer 2010)

Pen letters and poison

I turn off the quiet engine of the MG saloon and sit rooted to my seat, staring out of the passenger window. The view is depressing. I'm hoping that after today I will never have to come here again. I left this behind months ago. I cut it all from my life, so coldly, so abruptly, and until the cry for help, the midnight telephone call from such a familiar voice yet so far away, I would never have returned.

I should have. I know now I left this too late. I should have thought. I should have paid attention to those who loved me, then lost me. The people here have grieved for the warm, loving happy person I was, they will not recognise what is about to cross their threshold.

The small bungalow sits attached to two others. With one door, and one window it is hard to imagine from the outside how two people live comfortably on the inside. They have, and they do. For now. The people who reside here are a few of my closest relatives. They practically brought me up, gave a steady hand through my teens and early twenties, when my rebellious streak threatened to tamper with the hard stuff.

They brought me back, they showed me love, unconditionally, guidance, acceptance, they listened. I repaid them by running away and hiding my dirty secrets from them. I made the decision to remove them from my life rather than let them in and help to fix it. They were connected to a metaphorical dragon I had to slay. Casualties of war. Sitting here now, my heart full of love and pity for these people, brimming tears threatening to ruin my immaculate make up, I wonder just what mind have I that can forget so easily, that can turn and walk away from those I hold so close.

I touch the key in the ignition, indignation overpowering, I did the right thing. They didn't need what I may have to impart. They didn't need me. A burden. They didn't need the tarnishing, the reputation, the filth, the dirt that would have inevitably come if I had of stayed and faced the music. If I had sleighed just the one dragon, and walked through the seaside town my head held high, still it would not have been enough, to save their lives as they know them. I did the right thing. I am not infallible, however, and I know, that by protecting them, I ultimately protected myself. I'll tell myself whichever scenario I need to, to get through this. Maybe I should go.

Maybe I should leave, back to the small penthouse apartment in the middle of a city full of strangers. To my office. To my own thriving business, where I seldom feel the need to be personal. Trading antiquities and artefacts over a very successful online shop means very little human interaction. Apart from buying trips, and then of course, with my hand on the cash, and their minds on a profitable swap, I always have the upper hand.

I've become used to keeping people at a distance. Surrounded myself in a bubble no one should permeate. Keeping people at arm's length, never letting go the inner workings of my mind. I've become so adept at it the last six months; I've quite simply forgotten what my own favourite colour is. My favourite food, what I like to do. How I see the future. Day to day I live and work, and if truth be told, I'm thoroughly expecting not to have a future at all. I think I'm happy. As happy as I'll ever be.

One divorce under my belt, I have no desire to travel the romantic path again. When lust enters the building, my instincts leave twice as fast. I can't trust myself. It won't happen again.

It's a little secret between me and my stylist that evil events of my marriage turned my dark chocolate locks half grey. My marriage being the reason I ran away.

So now I'm back. I turn on the ignition and start to rev the engine. My temples are throbbing; my brain cannot cope with the memories. I need to flee, be somewhere else, someone else. I need a bath. I feel covered in grime. I shudder then involuntary dry heave. I have to go.

As I check in the rear view mirror before pulling out of the space, a sharp knock on my window startles me. My heart reaches my mouth, I instinctively reach into my hand bag for the illegal pepper spray and flick knife I've become used to carrying around. As I do, I look up, and see my step-grandfather, David. He's smiling unsurely through the glass.

I release my grip on my weapons and find a bottle of Xanex instead. My nerves are going to need a steadying if I am to get out of this car. I want to flee. I want to stamp my foot onto the accelerator and go, but the sadness behind David's eyes keeps me still. I lower the window, without turning off the engine.

"Come inside Ant, come inside, please."

My name is Antoinette. My parents thought being a big baby I'd be able to fight off the many bullies who would beat me up for their historical indulgence. They were wrong. It didn't kill me though – made me stronger, maybe so. Not strong enough.

"I don't think I can David. As long as everything's ok. I've seen you now. I've shown my face. I have to go."

"You CAN'T". David shouts urgency in his voice, and then looks around expecting curtains to twitch and a SWAT team to tackle him to the ground. I'm intrigued.

I turn the engine off. Usually such a gentle quiet man I'm worried. He must have reached the end of his tether a million times with the teenage Antoinette yet not once have I heard him raise his voice, or give anything close to an order.

I open the door, let my suited leg fall out, then with forced confidence, stand on my Jimmy Chou kitten heels and reach up to kiss David's grey stubble. He envelopes me in a bear hug. I've not being touched bodily, fully clothed or not since I left this shitty town behind six months ago. It's a strange feeling. Slightly awkward, but warm. He needs a shower. He smells of home.

"Thank you, thank you thank you. You are my last hope. Thank you so much. I didn't even know if you got my message. I didn't know I had the right number. So many people have called that number, but you've never returned the calls. We thought you were dead."

"I am David. Inside. This isn't about me though. I kept that old phone just in case. I've checked every message. You didn't need me in the others. You missed me and thank you for that, but in this one, you sounded so panicked. I had to come and see. I don't know what I expected; everything's exactly the same as I left it."

"I wish it were. I wish it were. I need to prepare you for what you are about to see."

"What?"

"Your Grandma. Your Grandma discharged herself from hospital this morning. She went in for her breathing, came out with this terrible pain. She's convinced they tried to kill her."

"Who tried to kill her?"

"The nurses, the doctors, who knows, she's delusional, anyhow, X-rays showed nothing. So she discharged herself. She has her nurse, but it's getting worse. I don't know what to do. I can't seem to help."

"So why am I here?"

"If you can convince her to go back to hospital, a nursing home, anything, please. I'll be forever in your debt. I'm sure it will save her life."

"Why would she listen to me? I'm sorry David, but there are many more people, lots of family. I'm not going to make one iota of difference." It's true; I can't see what good I will do, if anything, I'd just drag up the past. Selfishly, yes, my past, but still. That depth of emotion, my Gran doesn't need that by the sounds of it. She's spent the last ten years in and out of hospital. Refusing to give up smoking, her roll ups a natural extension of her third finger. Her emphysema threatens to win the battle, with my gran never quite giving up the ghost. This time will be no different.

"She loves you. She's been so worried. We really were beginning to think you'd died. We couldn't find you anywhere. Your gran was convinced she'd feel it though, if something had happened to you. She made excuses. After your marriage, she knew you needed time. She was hurt though, she wanted to help."

"I'm sorry. I'm here now. Let's just say I discovered a few things which sent me running for the hills. I couldn't bear to step foot in this place again."

"Not even a card? Not even to tell us you were ok? We've heard the rumours, we're not silly, and we think we are close to figuring out what sent you running the way you did."

"For your sakes David, I sincerely hope you're not."

I brush imaginary dust off my trouser thighs, and grab my Chanel handbag from the passenger seat of the car. Flinging it over my shoulder, I lower my winter sunglasses to my nose, flick my hair, then nod for David to follow me into his home.

He comes up close and reaches round me as I forget the knack of the back door handle, as he opens it swiftly, he whispers.

"You could never have known."

I know then that they do, they have figured it out, and still David is letting me into his home. Still he hugged me. Still he loves me. I'm overwhelmed, I don't remove the sunglasses.

I stride into the tiny kitchen. Expect to see my Gran with a stern look on her face, puffing out smoke from her wheelchair at the kitchen table. It's empty. Even the ashtray is empty. Dark, dismal. Cold. I shiver. This is not how I left things at all.

I hear a piercing scream and look to David for reassurance.

"Your Grandma is in a lot of pain Ant. She needs to be where they can give her round the clock care. I feel like I'm letting her down. I'm missing something."

"Ring the nursing home David. Ask them to send transport. With pain like that, I can't see Gran putting up much of a fight. I'll stay with her. Bedroom?"

David nods a sigh of relief as he ambles towards the phone. One eye still following me from the room. The bungalow smells old, of old people. Of brylcream and tweed perfume. Impulse and dettol.

Opening the bedroom door, I see a nurse first, a chubby nurse bending over the chest of drawers, filling a needle. She turns and smiles at me. Mouths, "I'm so sorry".

For what? What is she sorry for?

My Grandma's still here. I push the door a little wider, to see the feisty woman herself, and instead spy a shell of what once was. A deflated shell. Gran's nose looks like grey wax, already dead before the rest of her. I feel the Grim reaper is in the room with us checking his watch tapping his foot, like his own shroud he surrounds me, drapes me in a blanket of misery.

I find a bony hand from under the blanket, and hold it. It's cold. So cold, and hard.

Gran's eyes open. I remove my sunglasses. She squeezes my hand as tight as she possibly can.

"Antoinette, Antoinette, God answered my prayer. Thank goodness. Thank goodness, my beautiful girl. Now, will you see? They poisoned me!"

Chapter 2

I squeeze the cold hand a little tighter, and search my Grandmas wild eyes for some sign of insanity. There's panic, I see panic, but no madness. The nurse leans over us both and swiftly injects the contents of her needles into my Gran's wasted thigh. Gran doesn't flinch. As the nurse uses a sterile wipe to clean the entry point, the nurse whispers to me.

"Morphine, it can play with the brain. She's been shouting all day."

I'm pretty sure my Gran heard every word of it. Such a sharp mind, it's bound to be the last mortal attribute she lets go of.

The nurse packs a small bag, and begins to leave the room.

"I'll be back in four hours for meds and loo breaks ok. In the meantime, there's a red button, either that or ring me."

I nod, hurrying her out with my eyes. I want my Gran to speak to me.

"They poisoned me Ant. They did. You do believe me? I'm dying."

"I believe you Gran."

Just as Gran is about to talk again we hear bustles in the hallway, many people crammed into the miniscule bungalow, shouting, talking, as if we're not here. We're invisible.

A hefty Kathy Bates of a character pokes her head round the bedroom door and seems to look straight past the pair of us. I raise my eyebrows to Gran, who smirks in return.

I tighten my grip, as Kathy Bates speaks.

"Right, wheelchair, now, no fuss, get her on it, we'll wheel her to the nursing home. If Mohammed won't come to the mountain? Eh boys? Come on. Do it. Come on."

On her last words, two men, not boys, two pensionable men sweep in and swiftly grasp my frail shell of a grandmother under each armpit. She screeches and makes it awkward by refusing to let go of my hand. Kathy Bates tries to prise her fingers free. I'm not letting go either though.

"Leave her," I snap, "she doesn't have to let go. I'm not going anywhere."

Kathy turns and walks towards David, who is now stood in the doorway a pained expression on his face. Dastardly dog could not have played it better.

With a stage whisper she shouts quietly in his ear.

"We are doing this for her own good, tell your granddaughter. Was it not her who wanted her in a nursing home?"

"Yes it was," I interrupt, leaning awkwardly over Gran's wheelchair now, still holding onto her hand. Gran is wailing. There is no other word for it, except wailing, a continuous wail. It's loud, relentless, obviously pained.

"I didn't request it to the detriment of my grandmother's health though. She needs her family around her. She needs round the clock care. I assumed you'd be the best people for the job."

Kathy sticks out her chest. An impressive chest obviously used to her advantage in many a situation. Not here. Big boobs don't impress me.

"If you would let us do our job, we will. I am asking for one hour. To take her, get her settled in her room, with her medication, a drip, let the doctor see her, and then you can stay by her side for her entire stay."

A paranoid part of my mind flashes back to Gran's original panic. The poison. Was it these people? I shake my head to remove the delusional thoughts. We are in a sleepy seaside town. A town which yes, holds my many demons in the architecture, but staging this, going to this much effort to poison a defenceless old lady?

Ridiculous. I want to believe my grandmother; she's never lied to me before. However, one point sticks, the motive. Why would someone poison my Grandmother?

Jean Tilley, born 1926 to a wealthy family in the heart of Hertfordshire. Married at sixteen whilst with child, proceeded to produce a further eight children to the same man. Divorced 1978 swiftly followed b a remarriage to David, the gentlest man on earth. Televised shopping addict, filthy sense of humour, wasted genius mind.

It just doesn't make sense.

I follow the wheelchair and one of the man boys to the front door. Leaning down to kiss Gran I reassure her I will be just one hour. Not a second more. She grips my sleeve and almost spits into my ear. Frantic.

"The notes. Get the notes Ant. Kitchen drawer. In kitchen roll. Go now. Take them Ant hide them."

Kathy removes me and tries her best sympathetic smile as the man boy threatens to push the wheelchair straight through me. I move in a daze, I'm confused.

Gran's wails become louder as they load her into the back of a patient transporter.

"NOW Ant. GO NOW!"

The urgency spurs me to turn around and rush into the kitchen. The bungalow is empty. I don't know why, but I'm worried about even David finding me looking. Until I know what exactly Gran is talking about, I'm trusting my instincts and trusting no one.

I start in the larder, looking for kitchen roll. Under the sink, there are full rolls, nothing.

The drawer next to the sink sticks a little as I pull it out. I don't worry about the paintwork as I yank it. There's a rip and an old kitchen roll shows its cardboard holder in the jam of the door. I hear footsteps, pleasantries, a door creak, and rip the rest from the wood. Gran and her superglue, lethal combination. Without thinking, or looking at what I'm holding, I stuff it into my handbag, then shove the drawer closed with my foot, as I flick the kettle on and David sighs his way into the tiny kitchen.

"Cup of tea David?" I smile. He looks warn out. I feel momentarily guilty for robbing his home, but Gran's panic eases me.

"Antoinette, yes please. You will stay? You're not running now are you?" He asks.

"I'll stay as long as Gran needs me David. Let's just take one day at a time."

"The notes, did you get your Gran's notes?"

I want to lie about this, but my instincts tell me David is a good guy, that if given more time to explain, Gran would have done. I can't help but wonder though why David hasn't grabbed them before now, if they are so important.

"I did David. They're safe. I've not looked yet. What are they?"

"I'm ashamed to say I'm not sure. I think they're ramblings of an old woman. Your Gran refusing to let her mind give into old age would surround herself with books. Researching heaven knows what. You should know you helped with some of it. I lost interest. I don't believe in God or religion, and as most of her studies came back to the bible, I preferred to watch speedway whilst she scribbled and read."

It all comes back to me, not that many months before, sat on the floor of Gran's living room, papers everywhere, adding dates, researching events in history tying them to the bible, to the prophets, predictions.

"This research where we touched upon the world ending in 2021?"

"The very same."

"That was just rainy day ramblings. Like our rhyming treasure hunts. There was nothing serious there?"

"No, I wouldn't have thought so either, however your Gran alerted a lot of people when we became connected to the internet. She joined groups, forums I think, there were others that were really passionate about it. After you left she threw herself into it. She discovered more. Hidden meanings, warnings, lots of codes, reams and reams of numbers. I have the workings out in a big box. What you have there is the results. One is pretty useless without the other."

"Well, may I take the other?" I smile, it's not convincing. I hate myself for being so suspicious.

"Of course, take it. Put it in your car right now. I'll meet you at the nursing home; I just need to pack your Gran some things."

I feel guilty for my suspicions, but relief outweighs the emotion as David hands the box over. Only twenty minutes later I'm led up a musty seventies carpeted staircase, to a wood chipped yellow room. There's a pale green fifties teacup and saucer on the side of a wicker bedside table. Enamel sinks in one corner. The window is open, the stained nets blowing in the breeze. The view outside shows a launderette, happy shopper booze hall, a second hand clothes shop and a funeral home. I hate this town.

Gran is hooked up to a drip, her eyes are closed. She's breathing through her mouth, the oxygen up her nose. Her belly is huge under the pink satin quilted bedspread. I'm watching the teenagers with White Lightening cider outside the shops when I hear her speak.

"Come here Antoinette, I need you"

I move over to lie with her. I'm stroking her hair, holding her hand. I want to sob into her shoulder, for her to comfort me, like normal, but we're past that now.
"I'm scared Ant", says my gran, so quietly.
"What of gran?" I ask.
"Dying."
"Don't be silly gran, nothing to be scared of. The drugs you're on? Lennon would be proud!"
She smiles.
"It's the poison killing me Ant, until they take that away, the drugs will make it worse. I'm fighting them Ant."

"Gran, stop, let them work, let them do their magic, take the pain away. Get high legally! I'd join you if I could. Enjoy it. Once the pain's gone the doctors can find the problem. Fix it, and you can come home."
"I've tummy ache."
"As bad as the back ache?"
"No."
"You remember period's Gran? Pretend it's that."
She smiles, and then her whole body convulses with pain, she screams, loudly.
"I'm here Gran, I'm here."
Gran relaxes then gasps,

"Water..."
"I'll get it Gran, but I'm clumsy, I'll probably choke you..."
"I know you sod. Don't....care....."
I put the water into Gran's mouth; it's a sports bottle,
"Suck Gran, suck....I know you remember how".
She tries to laugh, and the water dribbles down her cheek, I wipe it away with a finger.
"Your skin, Antoinette, so soft, how?"
"Youth, Gran, youth." I laugh. She tries to move her arm to poke me, as she would've done, had she been better.
"Tell me a story," says Gran.
"About?"
"You, your last six months. Where've you been?"
"Away Gran, I had to get away. I'm so sorry."
"You're here now. Are you better for it?"
"I think I know what I have to do."
"What about work- money- your future?"
"Don't worry Gran, I'm a big girl now, I can take care of myself. I do ok."
"And love?"
"We'll see, two out of three ain't bad, eh?" I lean forward to whisper something in her ear.
"That's my girl" she says, as her eyelids droop.
She tightens her grip for a few seconds.
"I love you Antoinette, so so much. Thank you. Hold me, just one sleep, and we need to talk."
My face is wet with tears. I have so many questions, but Gran is exhausted.
Her voice trails off.
"You can do it Antoinette. You can lay your demons to rest, I'm so sorry, but I need you to fight mine as well. I'm so sorry Antoinette. Forgive me. There is no one else who understands. No one I can trust. Trust no one Antoinette. Promise me. Promise me."
Gran's body stiffens, I hold tighter, her grip becomes claw like, and she digs her nails into my hand. My head is buried in her hair, her scalp is cold. Her throat rattles, an involuntary horsey cough, and her hand falls onto the bed.
I slowly reach over to press the emergency button, once done, I go heavy with her.
I already know it's too late. My grandmother has just died in my arms.

Printed in Great Britain
by Amazon